This book is dedicated to Bandit, Flicker, Schnook, Caicos, Roger, Jack, Comet, Blue, and all the other bunnies who have enriched my life over the years. It is also dedicated to my parents, who I know are looking down on me, ever proud of their baby.

www.mascotbooks.com

ADVENTURES OF THE SUPER BUNNY CLUB

For more information, please contact:
Mascot Books
620 Herndon Parkway, Suite 320
Herndon, VA 20170
info@mascotbooks.com

Library of Congress Control Number: 2018907386

CPSIA Code: PRFRE1118
ISBN-13:978-1-68401-801-7

Printed in Canada

ADVENTURES OF THE SUPER BUNNY CLUB

DALE PERRY

ILLUSTRATED BY
PETER WILKS

CONTENTS

CHAPTER ONE

Once upon a time, at least according to the internet, there were four identical gray lop-eared bunnies that lived in four separate parts of the world:

Agent Rupert in Hungary

Dino in the Netherlands

Smurfy in Belgium

And a bunny named Blue in the United States.

You might think this story is going to be about the fact that these bunnies live in different places but all look the same. That is a very interesting story but not the one being told today. The story you are about to read is much more interesting and that is how these bunnies all became part of the Super Bunny Club.

You've never heard of the Super Bunny Club? I suppose it's not surprising because it is a network of *spy* bunnies who are united in protecting bunnies across the world. It turns out there are a lot of bad guys trying to steal bunny secrets and equipment and sometimes even their veggies, but you will read more about that later. Before we talk more about the spy activities of the Super Bunny Club, let's start by explaining how they all met.

There are a lot of things people don't know about bunnies and one of those things is that bunnies are very active on bunny social media. Especially on their PictoBun accounts. They mostly like to share pictures and videos of themselves doing cute things like sleeping, chewing, running, and doing binkies. In case you have never heard of binkies, these are very special bunny flips, hops, and in-the-air twists that bunnies perform only when they are very happy. Bunnies especially like to share their binkies online as even watching a good binky brings much joy to bunnies everywhere.

A bunny named Blue immediately created his PictoBun account the first night he came to live with his new mommy and daddy hoomins (that's what bunnies call humans...their spelling isn't always the best). This account was very important to Blue because he felt pretty alone and nervous in a new place, so making friends felt very necessary. He was also not really sure what he wanted to be when he grew up, so he thought looking at other bunnies' careers might give him some ideas. Blue signed on and started looking at pictures of other bunnies. He was surprised to see that there are very small bunnies, very big bunnies, very smooth bunnies, and very fluffy bunnies who live all over the world. They came in all different sizes, shapes, and colors, and they all seemed to have different hobbies and interests.

When Blue thought about his hobbies and skills, he felt that he might be skilled at eating treats, but in his heart he knew he was meant to do more with his life. In fact, one of his biggest dreams was to be a race car driver because he was very very very fast and he practiced all the time. In fact, his mommy and daddy could always hear him running very very very fast through the rooms upstairs practicing his laps. Sometimes his daddy would yell, "Blue what are you doing up there?" but Blue just kept going fast.

Blue put his thoughts of race car driving aside for a moment and continued to look at his PictoBun pictures. He immediately noticed that there was a bunny named Agent Rupert that looked just like him! In fact, they had the very same cage and were only born one day apart, but Rupert lived on the other side of the ocean. Agent Rupert referred to himself as a spy bunny in his profile and this was very intriguing to Blue as spy movies were some of his favorite movies to watch (bunnies like to watch a lot of movies in their downtime). Although Blue was currently dreaming of being a race car driver, the idea of combining careers was very appealing to him. Surely a race car driver bunny would be a good spy bunny as he was very very very fast so he could help to chase after bad guys.

Blue was new to making friends and a little shy but he was so intrigued by the idea of becoming a spy bunny that he couldn't resist reaching out. He sent Agent Rupert an instant bunny message asking if he too could become a spy bunny. He was surprised when Agent Rupert wrote back right away and told him that of course he could train to be a spy bunny. Blue explained his dream of becoming a race car driver and Agent Rupert agreed that he could use both a new spy bunny and a driver. Rupert explained that it is very important to have dreams and to never give up on them.

Agent Rupert, already being a very experienced spy bunny, asked if Blue knew how to use his cage as a teleportation device and this was a very new concept to Blue. Agent Rupert explained that late at night  bunnies can teleport to other bunny locations by harnessing power from their cages. Sometimes spy bunnies teleported to go on missions but, from the pictures he could see, it seemed to Blue many bunnies teleported to attend bunny parties with carrot juice and other treats but that seemed ok too. Rupert suggested that Blue could teleport over to Hungary that night so they could share some basil and get to know each other better. Because Blue's hoomins were asleep at night, this opened up a lot opportunities to teleport to meet his new friends.

Blue was pretty excited to teleport to Rupert's that night and to learn about all these new things, but then he started looking at PictoBun again and got a little distracted. But sometimes distractions are a good thing because suddenly, Blue found himself looking at another picture of himself! He was confused though because he didn't remember posting this picture of himself and his ears looked a little longer and he was pretty sure he didn't live in the Netherlands. So who was this pretty gray bunny with the slightly longer ears? "Dino." Blue read her name. *Her* name! Dino was a girl! There was another gray bunny out there who looked like Agent Rupert and Blue and she was a girl! Blue figured if two gray lop-eared bunnies were good then three must be better. Agent Rupert and Blue discussed and then reached out to Dino and asked her if she would be willing to become a spy bunny too. She agreed and suddenly there were three gray lop-eared spy bunnies.

They knew they needed a name for their spy club and it did not take them long to decide they would be called the Super Bunny Club. After all, they were all bunnies and they were all in the same club and they thought they were pretty super (bunnies tend to think pretty highly of themselves, especially when compared to hoomins). They told Dino that tonight would be the first official meeting of the Super Bunny Club at Agent Rupert's and she volunteered to bring some pellets to share, which made them even more excited. They would use this first meeting to get to know each other and to plan their first mission (while sharing some treats, of course).

While Blue, Rupert, and Dino were making plans together, suddenly a fourth gray lop-eared bunny named Smurfy sent Dino an instant message and asked if he too could join the Super Bunny Club. Dino, who always tried to be fair, suggested that there should be a vote and asked if he had any experience catching bad guys. Smurfy reported back that he had recently caught and expelled a carrot thief from his garden so the other members immediately voted him into the Club. They explained to Smurfy how cage teleporting worked and he said he would bring some fresh greens from his garden so now the bunnies were very excited indeed! Smurfy also had his own outdoor "castle" (which is what bunnies call their houses – they like to think they are very regal), so when the weather was nice the Super Bunny Club would be able to meet there too.

As Blue waited for his hoomins to go to sleep so he could teleport to Agent Rupert's, he sighed with happiness. He couldn't believe how lucky he was to have made friends so quickly from all over the world and, as a bonus, friends who were incredibly good looking (bunnies often think pretty highly of themselves). He also couldn't believe that he didn't have to give up his dream of being a race car driver, so he decided to himself that this would be the **First Rule of the Super Bunny Club: Never give up on your dreams.** And that, my friends, is how the Super Bunny Club was formed.

CHAPTER TWO

When Blue was finally confident that his hoomins were asleep, he closed his eyes and wished as hard as he could to teleport to Agent Rupert's house. He started to feel a buzzing around him and a giant **WHOOSH**. He opened his eyes and found himself staring at a black and white bunny who seemed not very surprised to see him, but Blue was certainly surprised to see him! Blue immediately thumped and flattened his ears (that is what bunnies do when they are scared) but the black and white bunny just kept eating his pellets and munching his hay and looked at Blue disinterestedly. "E-e-e-excuse me black and white bunny," he whispered "This is my first time teleporting and I was trying to go to Hungary to meet Agent Rupert." The black and white bunny kept chewing and with his mouth full said, "Well, you got the first letter of the place right but this is Hawaii and my name's not Rupert, my name is Mochi. Who are you?" Blue, now knowing that he did not seem to be in any danger, introduced himself and proudly announced that he was a race car driver AND a spy bunny AND a member of the Super Bunny Club. Mochi shrugged his shoulders (bunnies are not that impressed with other bunnies' career choices) and asked if Blue wanted some hay before he went to Hungary. Never being one to refuse food, Blue shared some hay with him but knew he had to get going as he didn't want to be late for the first club meeting. Mochi understood and gave him some dried pineapple for the trip and Blue once again closed his eyes, got into Mochi's cage, felt the buzzing and then **WHOOSH**, he was on his way again.

Blue was now really excited to meet the other gray lop-eared bunnies of the Super Bunny Club, but he looked around the room he landed in and he didn't see any bunnies at all. Suddenly, what appeared to be a large white dog hopped into the room. Wait, it was hopping. Was this a dog at all? His head was sort of shaped like a triangle and his ears! These were the most magnificent ears Blue had ever seen! In fact, this bunny's ears were so long he actually tripped over them while he was coming over to see who had landed in his living room. Blue put his ears back and thumped again as he was slightly afraid, but this dog-like rabbit certainly didn't feel afraid of him. "Hey little guy. What's up? My name is Lucas and I didn't know you were coming over to play but it's nice to have some company while my hoomins are sleeping." Blue sniffed the air tentatively. "Are you a rabbit?" asked Blue. The white rabbit proudly licked one of his ears that he was standing on and said, "I sure am. My name is Lucas and I am an English lop. You are probably noticing how long my ears are and how

big I am, but I am a rabbit just like you. Would you care for some carrot juice?"

Blue didn't know what was more impressive: this regal bunny and his amazing ears or the fact that he seemed to have his own supply of carrot juice. He would definitely have to talk to his mommy about that when he got home. Blue hesitated and said, "I really should be on my way. I am a new member of the Super Bunny Club and I was trying to teleport to Hungary." Lucas looked at Blue with confusion and told him that he had actually landed in New York City. He suggested Blue have a snack before he left because teleporting was not easy for a beginner bunny and he would need his energy. Blue shared some lettuce with Lucas and explained that he really did need to go, but that he would visit him again soon. He got into Lucas's cage, closed his eyes, felt the buzzing and **WHOOSH!**

Blue opened his eyes once again and found himself looking at a rather smallish light brown bunny wearing a buhnahnuh on his head. "Ahhh!" Blue screamed and quickly closed his eyes and tried to teleport out of there (nothing was quite as sceery as buhnahnuh to Blue and obviously the correct spelling is scary and banana, but bunnies sometimes spell things out they way they sound). Blue opened his eyes and was sad to discover that he was still in the same place but was relieved to see that the buhnahnuh wasn't real and seemed to be some kind of hat. Wait, a hat? Blue must have been talking out loud because the light brown bunny rolled his eyes. "Yes, this is a hat shaped like a banana. Do you have something to say about it?" Blue didn't know what to say exactly, but he still found the hat to be quite sceery so he quietly thumped and backed up a little. He was getting used to getting lost and meeting new bunnies at this point so he was a little less afraid (except for the sceery buhnahnuh hat). Blue didn't want to be rude though, so he gently asked if he was in Hungary. "No, you are in Japan." said the little bunny. "My name is Cooper and my mommy likes to post pictures of me on the internet wearing different hats. It was pretty embarrassing at first but I am famous now so I deal with it. It helps me to finance my life style." Blue backed up a little because the whole buhnahnah hat thing was still freaking him out but

he informed Cooper that he was trying to go to Hungary and was the newest member of the Super Bunny Club.

"Are you famous on the internet?" Cooper asked curiously. "I don't think so," Blue answered "but I probably will be soon because I am a race car driver AND a spy bunny." "Yes, but do you have any hats?" asked Cooper. Now Blue rolled his eyes. What was with this bunny and the hats? "I don't have a hat but I'm sure I will need disguises so perhaps I should get one." Cooper promptly volunteered to give Blue his banana hat but Blue wisely realized that he would stand out too much dressed like a buhnahnuh. "Um, I think I will need something a little less...obvious," said Blue and Cooper laughed, agreeing that a banana hat probably was a little bit much but that maybe it would scare away the bad guys. Blue kindly refused the hat again and ultimately settled on a Santa hat, which he figured might come in useful over the holidays. Cooper offered to share some tea with him and the two bunnies sat together and got to know one another. After sharing some tea and many more conversations about hats, Blue bid him goodbye, got into Cooper's cage, closed his eyes again, and the buzz and **WHOOSH!**

By now Blue was getting pretty tired of all this buzzing and **WHOOSHING** and not ending up where he needed to be for the meeting. This time he opened his eyes and froze. Busily destroying a cardboard box in front of him (bunnies love a good bit of bunstruction, which is what they call their activities when they destroy things in hoomins' homes) was a hairless bunny. No really, it had no hair except for a little bit on his ears and around his nose. "G'day mate," said the bunny jauntily and stared at him expectantly. "Um G'day?" Blue answered cautiously and then continued, "I don't suppose I would be in Hungary would I?" The hairless bunny stared at him curiously and said, "Noooo, you are in Australia. Sort of far from where you want to be aren't you? I'm Mr. B, what's your name?" Now Blue started to cry. He couldn't help it as big fat tears fell from his eyes. "Now, now. There, there," said Mr. B. "What's the matter?"

Blue explained that tonight was his first big meeting of the Super Bunny Club where he was supposed to become a true spy bunny and that he had been teleporting all over the world trying to get there. Mr. B was sympathetic and offered Blue some delicious grass from a place called "Outside." After snacking for awhile Blue got up the courage to ask what most people would want to ask a hairless bunny. "Mr. B," Blue started tentatively, "Can I ask? Why do you not have any fur?" "Huh? Oh fur. That's right. I forget some bunnies have that. Seems awfully annoying to me... all that shedding and cleaning. As for me, I was just born this way but I am a bunny through and through just like you. Now then, pick yourself up, concentrate really hard and I bet you will end up at your meeting in no time." Although Blue would have liked to stay longer, he was already very late so he thanked him for being so kind and for the grass, got into Mr. B's cage, closed his eyes, and concentrated really hard and then the buzz and **WHOOSH!**

Blue's eyes popped open and finally in front of him were three extremely good looking gray lop-eared bunnies who all looked exactly like him. He had made it! He was obviously a little late at this point (and full from all the snacks) but his tummy still rumbled when he saw all the treats that Agent Rupert, Dino, and Smurfy had provided for the first meeting. "I'm sorry

I'm late," Blue apologized. "You would not believe all the places I've been and all the bunnies I've met. One of them lived in Hawaii and one of them had HUGE ears and the other one wore a hat shaped like a buhnahnuh (at this point the Super Bunny Club looked very confused) and one of them had almost no hair at all! I never knew there were so many different kinds of bunnies in the world. They were all different from me but they were all kind and gave me food to eat (at this point the other bunnies looked a little jealous) and helped me to get back to my journey. These are all the buns we must work to protect!" Blue said excitedly. The Super Bunny Club clapped and binkied excitedly. Blue then explained that he had created a rule for the club and now, based on his adventures that evening, felt he had another one to add. The other bunnies agreed that they should have some rules to follow, so Blue proudly declared the **Second Rule of the Super Bunny Club: Even if we look different, we're all the same inside so we need to treat each other with love and respect.**

CHAPTER THREE

After the Super Bunny Club finished getting to know one another, Agent Rupert thumped his hind legs and Blue, Dino, and Smurfy stopped mid-chew to pay attention to his announcement. "Super Bunny Club members – welcome to the world of being a spy bunny!" With this all the bunnies cheered and binkied (remember, binkies are what bunnies do when they are very happy) and it took them awhile to calm down after that. Agent Rupert thumped again and the bunnies quickly came to order. "As I said, welcome to the world of being a spy bunny." At this point Smurfy did a small binky, but so small you could hardly notice it. "The work you have signed up to do is dangerous. There are bad guys everywhere and many problems to be solved and it is our job to protect others from harm and wrong-doing. Our enemies may be big or small. They may be other animals or they may be hoomins. We must be prepared for anything."

At this point Blue started day-dreaming a little bit about driving his race car during spy missions, but Agent Rupert cleared his throat and Blue gave a little jump. "As I was saying, we must be prepared for anything and tonight my friends, is one of those nights." At this news, the Super Bunny Club tingled with excitement. "It has been reported to me that one of our dear friends, Akil, has always thought he was living with another bunny but he may actually be living with (here he paused dramatically, something bunnies loved to do)... a hoomin. We have been called to his home to figure out who takes care him this very evening."

At this the Super Bunny Club looked at each other in confusion. Weren't hoomins always the caretakers of bunnies? It seemed that they were assigned to clean up after them and to provide shelter, food, water and, most importantly, treats. As if reading their minds, Agent Rupert reported that Akil was a young and rather inexperienced bun who may simply not understand the difference between bunnies and hoomins. Helping him to understand without scaring him could be the trickiest part of their mission. This was still all a little confusing to Blue, but he knew he needed to act strong and unafraid if he really wanted to grow his career as a spy bunny. He swallowed deeply and his voice rang out, "We are ready Agent Rupert! Lead us to the home of this bun Akil and we will be prepared to assist in any way necessary!" And then, a little more quietly added, "But can you please be in charge of the teleporting because it didn't go so well last time." The rest of the Super Bunny Club tittered with laughter, but Blue didn't mind because he knew they loved him just as he was and besides, teleporting wasn't as cool as driving a race car anyway. With that, Agent Rupert gathered all the bunnies in his cage, asked them to close their eyes, and then buzz and **WHOOSH!** They were off.

The Super Bunny Club all opened their eyes slowly and immediately noticed that it was very hot where they were. Quite hot as a matter of fact, and when Agent Rupert checked the map on his phone he determined that they were in Egypt. "Egypt!" cried Dino. "Don't they make mummies out of bunnies in Egypt?" At this the rest of the Super Bunny Club looked quite concerned when a small white bunny with pretty blue eyes peeked out at them from behind a sofa. "He-he-he-hello," Akil said nervously. "Would you happen to be the Super Bunny Club?" Smurfy replied that indeed they were the Super Bunny Club (at which he gave a little binky of joy, still not able to fully contain his excitement at his newfound job). "We understand that you are not sure who you are living with Akil and that it's making you quite nervous," said Agent Rupert kindly. "We're here to help you solve the mystery, but first we need to see where your caretaker currently is located in this apartment so we can fully prepare ourselves."

Akil informed them that his caretaker was sleeping in the living room so the Super Bunny Club all quietly hopped to the hallway and peeped around the corner where they saw something underneath a blanket, clearly sound asleep. "Hm-mmm, this will require the use of an extravagant disguise."

Agent Rupert declared. At this statement there were many binkies of joy because bunnies love a good disguise and they felt fortunate that they would get to wear one on their very first mission. The bunnies all agreed that the best disguise would be to dress like a hoomin in case the thing on the couch woke up. Akil quickly gathered some clothing, a hat, and some sunglasses that were in the apartment so the Super Bunny Club could put together their disguise. They quickly realized that everything was too big for them.

"Since these items are all too big for us, we will obviously need to make ourselves the same size as a hoomin so we can wear them." Blue wasn't sure how they were going to do this but he didn't love the idea of making himself hoom-in-sized. His race car was already custom made for him so if he got bigger, he wouldn't be able to fit in it. Agent Rupert once again thumped, bringing Blue out of his daydream. "Here is what we will do. To avoid being detected, we will stand up on our hind legs and then stand on one another's shoulders, at which point we should be tall enough to put on this coat and sunglasses. Akil, you may have to put the hat on as the final touch." This all sounded a little treacherous to the Super Bunny Club members, but since they were new and because they were excited to wear a disguise, they quickly agreed. It was decided that Agent Rupert would stand on top and wear the hat and sunglasses and that Dino would be underneath him to work the arms. Smurfy would come next as he was strong and would provide a solid foundation, and Blue would be on the bottom and work the legs as he was the fastest and could help them get away quickly. Blue was disappointed that the plan did not, at least yet, include a race car but he was happy they recognized his speed.

Akil hopped and danced excitedly back and forth in front of the group as they donned their costume and once they were dressed, he looked at Agent Rupert and asked, "Um, now what?" Frankly, Agent Rupert wasn't sure what they were going to do next as he too had gotten caught up in the excitement of a disguise. He was an experienced spy bunny though and a quick thinker, so he quickly decided the group would walk/ hop into the living room, get close to the thing sleeping on the couch and gently peel back the blanket to see if Akil's caretaker was a bun or hoomin. "How will you know?" Akil asked nervously, but Agent Rupert promised him they would reveal their technique after further inspection.

Agent Rupert peered down into the coat to see that the rest of the Super Bunny Club were ready to go. Dino nodded in nervous agreement, Smurfy gave a paws up, and Blue revved his engines (well, in his mind he revved his engines but in reality he really just blinked nervously). "Then let's go Super Bunny Club! We're off to investigate!" Akil ran back behind the couch as the Super Bunny Club teetered and tottered into the living room. Halfway across the room the group suddenly came to a stop and looked down at Blue, who had found a small piece of hay and decided he was little hungry so he stopped to eat it. "AHEM." Agent Rupert cleared his throat quietly but with authority and they were on their way again. It had been agreed that Dino, as she was the arms of the team, would be the one to gently pull back the blanket while Smurfy would use his binoculars to get a better view and Blue would get them in the right position to flee if necessary.

Quietly, Dino leaned forward and grabbed the blanket with her teeth and slowly dragged it away from the lump on the couch who snored gently. Once the face was revealed Smurfy was able to get a better look and with no fur, strange ears, and some kind of hair growing on its face, he quietly but definitively declared the lump to be a man hoomin. At this moment, the lump of hoomin started to turn over and slowly opened his eyes and then closed them again and then opened them again as he stared into the sunglasses of Agent Rupert who was peering closely at him. "Run, Blue, run!" they yelled and Blue, waiting for this moment all evening, took off running, leaving the rest of them one bunny shorter and still standing in front of the hoomin. Thankfully at this moment, Akil came bounding into the room and jumped onto the chest of the man hoomin and the rest of the Super Bunny Club scattered, leaving their coat, sunglasses, and hat behind.

The Super Bunny Club hid behind some cushions and after a bit of time, Akil hopped back into the room quietly and informed the spy bunnies that the lump had fallen asleep and had muttered something about a bad dream. "Wh-wh-what did you find out Agent Rupert?" Akil asked nervously. "Smurfy, since you had the binoculars and had the best view, please tell Akil exactly what you saw." Smurfy was honored at being given such a big task and swallowed nervously in hopes that he would get his summary right. "Well Akil, with the use of our super spy binoculars, I was able to get a good look and it's important for you to know that your caretaker is definitely a man hoomin." Akil looked a little startled but Smurfy quickly continued. "This is very very good news Akil. You see, most bunnies have hoomin caretakers and we have learned over time and through much trial and error, that hoomins are very easily manipulated and will give you food and water, clean your cage, and if you get really good at bossing them around, will give you lots of treats." "I…I…I…don't know if I will be brave enough to do that," Akil said nervously. Agent Rupert and Dino were quick to point out that Akil was already manipulating his hoomin quite nicely as he had a nice clean cage, fresh greens, water, and occasional treats. This made Akil feel a little better about things, and he thanked the Super Bunny Club for helping him figure out this mystery and invited them back any time for a bunny party at his house. With that, the Super Bunny Club got into Akil's cage, closed their eyes, and then the buzz and **WHOOSH!**

When they opened their eyes again they were back at Agent Rupert's house in Hungary. Agent Rupert looked expectantly at his new recruits and asked them what they had learned. "I know! I know!" Blue shouted a bit too loudly as a small poop popped out of him. Dino and Smurfy giggled but Blue didn't even notice. "Yes, Blue. Go ahead," said Agent Rupert kindly and ignoring the poop. He knew Blue was just terribly excited about the mission they had returned from and besides, with bunnies, sometimes poop just happens. "Well, when we first heard about the mission none of us thought it made much sense because it seemed pretty obvious that it was likely a hoomin taking care of Akil. But then, once we got there, we all saw how young and nervous Akil was about his situation, so the right and kind thing to do was to help him even if we didn't really understand why he was upset." The rest of the Club agreed and huddled together with Blue to determine what lesson they had learned from this mission. After some discussion Blue proudly announced the **Third Rule of the Super Bunny Club: Always be ready to help others, even if you don't understand why they are upset.**

CHAPTER FOUR

After such a long night of traveling (some of which was not intentional) and his first successful spy adventure, Blue was pretty exhausted. It seemed he was the only one though because the rest of the Super Bunny Club was still filled with energy and binkies galore. "Come on Blue," prodded Dino. "It's time for a Super Bunny Club house party!" Blue didn't exactly know what a party was, but he sensed that it would involve treats and snacks. He heard a shaking noise coming from the other room and thumped thinking that perhaps a bad guy had followed them back to Agent Rupert's, but when the noise kept going and no one else seemed concerned, he tentatively hopped around the corner. He found Agent Rupert shaking a metal canister that seemed to have ice and something liquid in it. "Care for some carrot juice, Blue?" Agent Rupert asked. Blue had never had carrot juice but it sounded like something he might like and the sprig of basil poking out of the glass in front of him made it that much more appetizing. He cautiously

took a sip and found that it was incredibly delicious and immediately asked for more but stirred this time instead of shaken.

Agent Rupert happily refilled Blue's glass while Smurfy came by and asked if there was anything else to drink. "Hmmm," thought Agent Rupert, "How about a basil smoothie?" "Yum!" cried Smurfy and binkied around the room. Agent Rupert got to work blending the smoothie and Dino turned on some music so they could dance (bunnies love to dance almost as much as they like to binky but very often the two seem to almost be the same thing). While Blue had enjoyed his carrot juice, he was still very hungry after this evening's adventures and inquired if he might have some treats. Agent Rupert cut him up a small piece of apple which the rest of the Super Bunny Club polished off, and they started nosing around the room to see if there were even more treats to share. Soon Dino found a bag of hay and tore it open gleefully, spreading hay all over the room. The bunnies were very excited for both the hay and the mess (because bunnies love nothing more than a good mess) and soon they were dancing around with not a care in the world. If this was part of being a spy bunny, thought Blue, this was going to be more fun than work.

THUNK came the noise from outside. Blue glanced toward the sliding glass doors, but all he could see was his reflection and he paused to notice just how cute and good looking he was. "What are you looking at Brother?" asked Smurfy as he hopped next to

Blue. The Super Bunny Club members almost immediately started calling each other Brother and Sister for their bond was that strong and their resemblance to one another led them to believe that they clearly must be related and perhaps just separated at birth. "Well," said Blue perplexedly, "I thought I heard something outside but maybe it was just the dancing." Smurfy, now also noticing how good he looked reflected in the glass door, shrugged and went back to the party.

Blue, after some rest, decided he was ready for some more treats, and as he was hopping away, heard the noise again. THUNK. This time he looked out the door and thought he could see a flashlight but Dino had turned on the disco ball (yes, bunnies have disco balls) so it was rather hard to see outside. "Agent Rupert, is it possible that someone could be in your backyard?" asked Blue. "Oh, I doubt it Blue. We have a fence, which my hoomins think will keep me from running away because they clearly don't know that a fence is nothing for a spy bunny, so I'm sure it's nothing. It's probably just the disco ball and the binkying you're hearing." Agent Rupert then hopped back toward the cord he had just discovered (bunnies *love* to chew on cords, which is obviously very dangerous but bunnies are also not very good at avoiding temptation). Finally, Blue decided it must just be his imagination and settled down to take a little nap. Just as he was closing his eyes he heard the THUNK again but ignored it because he was tired and no one else seemed to be worried about it. Besides, they had already worked hard today and it seemed that the Super Bunny Club must be off duty. The other bunnies, with their tummies overly full, soon grew tired as well and began nodding off to sleep.

The bunnies were all almost asleep when Agent Rupert's phone began to ring (most bunnies have phones to access their PictoBun accounts and keep in touch with one another). Agent Rupert snapped to attention, as did the rest of the other bunnies, because the serious ring tone was rather loud and disruptive. Agent Rupert's eyes widened as he prepared to take the call. "Brothers and Sister! Quick! To attention! And put those glasses away quickly! This is a call from none other than the Presibun himself, George Washingbun!" With that, poop popped out of all three bunnies as they scattered to push the party debris out of the way. Agent Rupert rolled his eyes a little, because he knew his hoomins were not going to be happy about the poop, and answered the call. The Presibun looked very serious as the Super Bunny Club gathered around the screen. "I see you have finally assembled the rest of your spy bunny team," George Washingbun said approvingly. "Yes Sir, Mr. Presibun. What you see before you is the very best of the best. In fact, they had their first spy mission tonight in Egypt and helped a scared little bun understand that he was well-loved by his hoomin. We even got to wear a disguise!" The Presibun's eyes widened a bit at the mention of a disguise because he too greatly appreciated a good disguise. "Well done, Super Bunny Club. Well done. I have come to you with another urgent mission tonight so I hope you are up for the challenge." The Super Bunny Club stared side-eyed at one another a little guiltily as they were actually now quite tired from the long night and the bun house party. "We stand ready to serve Mr. Presibun," piped up Dino, as girl bunnies were never very much intimidated by authority figures. "That's excellent," said George Washingbun, "because there has been a great carrot heist!"

Three of the bunnies inhaled with shock, but Blue was a little confused. "What's a heist?" Blue whispered to Dino (because girl bunnies also always seemed to know what big words mean…). "A robbery!" Dino exclaimed breathlessly as Blue now sucked in his breath in shock as well. There was much thumping and whispering until the Presibun cleared his throat and began to speak again. "This evening, at several sites across the area, it seems that bad guys have been breaking into the gardens of unsuspecting bunnies and stealing the carrots from their hoomins' backyards. We are not exactly sure how they are managing to do all of this at the same time, but it must be an extremely large group of bad guys. I hope you can help."

Dino seemed to be deeply lost in thought as Agent Rupert replied, "Have no fear Mr. Presibun. The Super Bunny Club is up for the adventure and will catch these bad guys before you can say carrot juice!" With that, Agent Rupert gave a little hiccup, as he had clearly had a little too much carrot juice and had a bit of a stomach ache. "Keep me posted Super Bunny Club. George Washingbun out." And with that George Washingbun dropped his phone on the table in front of him but nothing happened. He blinked curiously as Smurfy whispered, "Mr. Presibun, you have to click off the video screen."

"Uh, oh. Right. Georgewashingbunout!" he said quickly and clicked off the screen. The Super Bunny Club looked at each other with some embarrassment. They were full, tired out from binkying and dancing and had definitely put fun before work for a good part of the night. "I have an idea," Blue said timidly. The three other bunnies looked at him curiously. "It seems this might be a good time to have another rule of the Super Bunny Club." And with that, Blue proclaimed the **Fourth Rule of the Super Bunny Club: Everything in moderation. There is a time for fun and a time for work, but they must be balanced for you to accomplish all your goals.** The rest of the Super Bunny Club nodded their heads in agreement and quickly cleaned up the apartment and got back to work.

CHAPTER

FIVE

The first thing the Super Bunny Club did after cleaning up after their house party was to go outside to inspect the garden. Blue felt a little silly for not following his gut and going out there earlier every time he heard a THUNK, but he was also a little afraid of the dark, if he was honest (not that he would ever admit that out loud because bunnies seldom admit to weakness or wrongdoings, for that matter). Sure enough, there were gaping holes in the ground where carrots had previously been growing. At that moment the whole Club felt a little guilty for letting this happen right outside of where they were gathered. Blue started hopping around the garden to see if anything else was missing, stopping every few hops to take a little bite of veggie here and there, until Agent Rupert cleared his throat and Blue thumped back into attention.

"What doesn't make sense is how carrots disappeared from multiple locations at the same time," Agent Rupert pondered. "Surely, there can't be that many bad guys all working together but I'm not sure how all of this could have happened simultaneously if that wasn't the case." At this, Dino hopped forward. "Agent Rupert, I don't think you are thinking through all the possibilities," Dino said politely. "We live in a world where you can do almost anything with technology. Maybe it is possible that there is one bad guy but he is using different devices to suck these carrots out of the ground. I would suggest that we talk to a bunny I know who might be able to help us with some computer support. His name is Cashew and he is excellent with technology and I bet he could figure it out." Agent Rupert smiled. "Of course I know Cashew," he said. "It might be good to invite his friend Secret Macadamia as well, as he is truly the master of disguises and could teach us more about that as well." The bunnies all tittered excitedly at the mention of disguises and they were anxious to bring on their new recruit. Smurfy raised his paw and volunteered to teleport to Cashew and Secret Macadamia to fetch them. Blue was secretly relieved that he didn't have to try teleporting again, especially when his belly was so fully of treats. With that, Smurfy jumped into Agent Rupert's cage, closed his eyes, and then the buzz and **WHOOSH**. He was gone.

The rest of the Super Bunny Club headed back into the apartment and were thinking about a little snack when **WHOOSH!** All of a sudden, Smurfy was back with Cashew. They hopped out of Agent Rupert's cage and Rupert explained the situation to their new arrival. Cashew paused for a moment and then said, "Wait just one minute. Let me consult with Secret Macadamia to see what he thinks." With that Cashew ran around in circles for a few minutes and darted underneath the couch where only his nose could be seen peeking out. "What on earth is he doing?" Blue whispered not unquietly. From underneath the couch come the pronouncement. "It is I, Secret Macadamia! As you can see, I'm the Master of Disguises and I am here to assist with your problem. I understand you need technical support."

Blue rolled his eyes (and yes, bunnies like to roll their eyes but sometimes only other bunnies can tell when they are doing that). "Um, we can see you Cashew!" Blue called out and the bunny underneath the couch didn't reply. "Hello! We totally saw you run under the couch!" Blue cried out a little louder. He looked confusedly at Agent Rupert who just smiled while Dino and Smurfy didn't seem to be bothered by any of this either. "Am I missing something here? That clearly is Cashew under the couch. There is no Secret Macadamia. How on earth is a crazy bunny like this going to help us?" While Blue was talking, Cashew/Secret Macadamia had crawled away from the couch and was now sitting right behind Blue. "Ahem." said Cashew quietly.

Blue whirled around, gave a disbelieving look to Cashew and said, "Cashew. Enough games. There is no Secret Macadamia. That was just you running under the couch and pretending to be someone else. Frankly, it's not even a very good disguise." "Isn't it?" Cashew/Secret Macadamia questioned. "Perhaps right now you are looking at Secret Macadamia and not Cashew because his disguise is so perfect." Blue rolled his eyes again but paused when Agent Rupert looked at him seriously. "Think about it, Blue. Do you really know that this isn't Secret Macadamia? It could be. After all, the four of us in the Super Bunny Club look identical. Wouldn't you be confused if I said I was really Dino? Or Smurfy? Sometimes the best disguise is the most obvious one. In fact, that gives me an idea for a future training mission," Agent Rupert said.

While the new spy bunnies wondered what their new future training exercise would be, Cashew (or was it Secret Macadamia?) pondered the carrot disappearances. "It could be..." Cashew paused for dramatic effect ."Yes?" exclaimed the Club. "What do you think it is?" Cashew ignored them, humming silently to himself. "No. No. That's probably not it at all." "Oh." said the bunnies sadly in unison. "Then again, I suppose if I really think about it carefully it could also be..." Cashew paused dramatically once more and immediately noticed that this dramatic pausing was not going to work much longer as the bunnies were shifting with boredom and losing interest.

He quickly asked to see the garden where the carrots had been taken from, and once outside, he ran as quickly as he could behind the shed and then hid under a broom that was propped up against the wall. "Here we go again," Blue thought to himself. Sure enough, Smurfy hopped up to Cashew/Secret Macadamia and addressed him as Cashew, to which the bunny under the broom replied, "It is not Cashew! It is I, Secret Macadamia, come to solve the problem." Blue immediately turned and began eating some basil that was growing nearby because he already knew how this was going to play out. Smurfy was very respectful though and asked Secret Macadamia if he knew how all the carrots were disappearing. Secret Macadamia looked quite pleased with himself and said, "I'm surprised you bunnies haven't figured it out yet but it's quite obvious to me. Clearly this theft has been carried out by much larger versions of the Giant Sucking Machine (this is what bunnies call vacuum cleaners). My guess is that they are operated by drones from a Central Command Center and are programmed to simultaneously suck up the carrots and return them to the evil mastermind carrying out this plot."

Smurfy thumped at the naming of the Giant Sucking Machine and Blue ran and hid under the steps. Dino and Agent Rupert, who had successfully encountered and battled this Machine before, just pondered the idea. Agent Rupert turned to address the group and standing behind him was Cashew. At least he thought it was Cashew. "Um, Secret Macadamia? That is truly an incredible deduction! How did you ever think of it?" Cashew looked back at Agent Rupert and said, "I'm Ca-

shew, not Secret Macadamia. Did you actually see him? He's often so well-disguised that you wouldn't even recognize him." With this Blue came out from underneath the steps shaking his head. He couldn't sit through this again. "Perhaps we can move on to trying to figure out how to stop the Machine instead of worrying about who said it." Agent Rupert gave Blue a stern look because he was being a little rude and said, "That is an excellent idea Blue. What did you have in mind?" Blue immediately knew he had been a little too full of himself and stepped back. "I was suggesting that we all think about it together Agent Rupert. As a new spy bunny I don't have all the answers yet but I would like to volunteer to drive the race car if one should be needed." The bunnies all giggled at the idea of Blue chasing around a Giant drone-operated Sucking Machine in a race car, but then remembered how serious the situation was and began to think.

Bunnies think best when they are snacking, so they decided to use the opportunity to fill their bellies a bit, though Blue's was already pretty full, and thought and thought and thought and ate and ate and ate. Finally, Smurfy raised his head and

said, "Maybe we can lay a trap for the Giant Sucking Machine? As you know, I have previously caught a bad guy stealing carrots from the garden near my outdoor castle but I didn't tell you how I did it. I tied a string around the bottom of a carrot, put it back in the ground and when the bad guy tried to take it out, the string rang a bell at my castle and he was scared and ran away and hasn't come back." The group agreed that this was a very good idea indeed and Dino added on to it. "What if we tie strings to several of the carrots and when the Giant Sucking Machine comes, we can pull on the strings and yank it out of the sky! The only thing I'm worried about is that we might not be strong enough."

At that, Blue began binkying around the garden with much glee. Cashew (er, Secret Macadamia) and the rest of the group looked at Blue curiously. He went faster and faster and faster and finally stopped. It was Secret Macadamia who figured it out. "Ah yes, I see! Well played Blue. We can tie the strings to Blue's race car and when the Giant Sucking Machine comes, he can drive away at top speed and yank the drone right out of the sky!" All the bunnies were so excited by the idea that they all began binkying (with a bit of pooping here and there) and cheered and chattered with excitement.

While they were binkying, Cashew ran into the house and stuck his head out the door. "Friends!" he said. "It is I Secret Macadamia and I will help you to implement this plan!" Blue didn't even care that this whole Cashew/Secret Macadamia strangeness was going on again because he was going to his race car on a mission. And besides, Cashew had just helped to make it happen, so he must not be that bad. But before the rest of the Super Bunny Club could go into the house, Blue paused thoughtfully at the top of the steps and turned to face his brothers and sister. "Brothers and Sister," he said, "I have come to a realization. This whole time I have found the whole Cashew/Secret Macadamia thing to be quite odd and might have even been a little rude about it. The problem is that I assumed there was something wrong with Cashew without getting to really know him and Secret Macadamia. Throughout the night, however, I've come to realize they both possess an important set of skills so assuming he was crazy without knowing him wasn't the nicest or smartest thing to do." Blue now looked like he was going to cry so Dino snuggled up beside him and gave him a big lick on the nose. "Perhaps it is time for another rule Blue?" Blue blinked back his tears and looked with love on his fellow spy bunnies. "Yes! I now announce the **Fifth Rule of the Super Bunny Club: Never assume anything about anyone. Get to know them first!**" With that all the bunnies zoomed into the house to catch up with Cashew. Er, Secret Macadamia.

CHAPTER

SIX

After discussing their plans, the Super Bunny Club saw that it was starting to get light out and that the night was turning into day. They decided to teleport back to their own cages to get some rest for the next night's mission and to gather up the supplies they needed from their hoomins. The bunnies were all exhausted, so the day went by quickly and before they knew it they were all teleporting back to Agent Rupert's house and even Blue made it without a problem. There wasn't a lot of chitchat between the bunnies as they didn't know when the Carrot Thief would strike so they needed to work quickly. Smurfy had found some strings and Dino had found some clips so they could attach the ropes securely to Blue's race car. The bunnies headed outside and began to pull some of the biggest and ripest carrots out of the ground and attached the strings to the bottoms as tight as they could.

Once all the knots were tied, the bunnies all looked expectantly at Blue for it was time to attach the strings to his race car. "Ok, Blue. We're ready to tie the strings to your race car!" Dino said excitedly. At this, Blue began running around the garden in circles very very very fast. So fast that he was just a blur to the other bunnies. When Blue stopped, the spy bunnies all clapped and cheered and now it was Cashew's turn to look confused. "Um, excuse me. But am I the only one who has realized that Blue does not actually own a race car?" Blue's eyes immediately filled with tears and Dino, his ever faithful sister, stepped forward and said, "Cashew. Much like we don't question the appearance and disappearance of Secret Macadamia, we also don't question Blue's race car. He believes he can be a race car driver and is clearly very very very fast. So fast, in fact, that he was just a blur to all of us which is why we didn't even notice his race car." Smurfy jumped in to support the argument and said, "To be on the safe side, I suggest we tie the strings to Blue just in case he needs to eject from his race car. This way we will still be able to pull the drone from the sky." The other spy bunnies all nodded seriously in agreement and Blue beamed with happiness at them for supporting his dream of being a race car driver. Cashew/Secret Macadamia simply nodded with understanding, for he could understand the importance of encouraging and accepting another's dreams even if they didn't make sense to him.

It was fully dark now and a moonless night, so the bunnies were well-hidden behind the garden shed. Blue was flat to the ground with the strings tied around his middle and ready to spring into action. He was so focused, in fact, that he didn't even notice when the other bunnies decided to share a midnight snack of some of the smaller carrots they had "accidentally" pulled. He knew he was critical to this mission and he wasn't going to do anything to let down his fellow bunnies. "Shhhh. Listen!" said Cashew. The bunnies all got quiet and listened with their ears forward. They all heard a grumbling noise but then suddenly it stopped. They decided it must not have been the drone when they heard the grumbling again. "It sounds so close to us!" Smurfy said a little nervously. Once again the grumbling stopped and once again they began eating their carrots. This time the grumbling was much louder and Dino thumped in reaction! Agent Rupert winked at the other bunnies and hopped over to where Blue was crouched and waiting. "Are you hungry, Blue?" Blue responded embarrassedly, "Um, what makes you ask that, Agent Rupert?" Having realized the grumbling they were hearing was merely Blue's empty tummy, Agent Rupert encouraged him to keep up his fuel for the mission and have a bite or two of carrot. Blue appreciated that no one teased him about his rumbly tummy but only ate a few bites and quickly got into position again.

A few long minutes later, the bunnies heard a sound that was definitely not Blue's tummy. It was a high-pitched whining sound and they all thumped in unison when they heard it. Out of the darkness, they could make out a dark shape getting closer and closer to the garden, and as it got lower to the ground, several long tubes appeared and the bunnies could hear the sound of the Giant Sucking Machine. "Be ready, Blue!" they all said at the same time and Blue flexed his muscles and prepared to take off in his race car. The noise got even louder as the Giant Sucking Machine identified the biggest and juiciest carrots (which thankfully had strings tied to them) and the noise became more of a roar as the carrots slowly started to rise out of the ground. "Be ready, Blue!" they all said again but just then Blue felt the strings go tight and began to run. At first he felt like he didn't have any traction and was stuck in one place. Thankfully, all of a sudden, he heard a voice whispering in his ear, "It is I Secret Macadamia and I am here to assist with your problem!" With that, Blue felt a push from behind and the ground grip beneath his paws and he began to run. He felt a little slow at first but when he felt the wind in his ears and the strings pull even tighter he had a burst of speed like he had never felt before! Soon he ran out of the garden, down the road and was almost at the end of the street when he heard a crash and BOOM! Suddenly, the drone and the carrots were on the ground and the rest of the spy bunnies caught up and all binkied with joy that their plan had worked!

Blue looked around and went up to Secret Macadamia to thank him for the push but Cashew just stared back and said, "What are you talking about? It's me Cashew. I haven't seen Secret Macadamia for awhile now." As hard as Blue tried, he was still struggling with this whole idea of two bunnies in one but he simply said, "Oh. Well if you happen to see him, tell him thank you." Cashew smiled with gratitude and at that moment, a special friendship was formed between the two and they quickly joined the other bunnies in their joyful binkying.

CHAPTER SEVEN

The bunnies wasted no time dragging the drone back to the garden and quickly untied all the carrots (which they may or may not have eaten). Thankfully, Cashew was there with all of his computer knowledge, and it wasn't long before he had hooked up his phone to the drone's computer and was downloading data. The bunnies anxiously circled around Cashew waiting to see the GPS coordinates of the drone's home so they could find the Carrot Thief. "Um, Agent Rupert? What exactly are we going to do when we get the address of the thief?" Blue asked nervously. "We will have to discuss as a group to see what everyone thinks, Blue, and then we will come up with a plan." With this Blue looked very concerned. He had already driven his race car and felt he had contributed a lot to the mission and was afraid he was now out of ideas. Agent Rupert looked kindly at him. "Don't worry, Blue. I can throw in some of my ideas from previous missions to help us brainstorm." Blue inwardly sighed with relief. He felt very fortunate to be working with such a kind and knowledgeable spy bunny.

Suddenly, Cashew looked up and the bunnies stared expectantly. "Very interesting. It could be…" Cashew paused, again for dramatic effect. "Yes!?" exclaimed the Super Bunny Club. "What do you think it is?" Cashew hummed silently to himself. "No. No. That's probably not it at all." "Oh," said the bunnies sadly in unison. "Then again, I suppose if I really think about it carefully it could also be…" Before Cashew could drag it on any longer, Dino jumped in because she was really anxious to catch this thief. "Did you find out where the drone came from and where the Carrot Thief is, Cashew?" Cashew again paused, but sensing the bunnies growing frustration with his dramatic pauses he quickly got right to the point. "The Carrot Thief is…" He couldn't help inserting a small pause. "Apparently right down the road in the old barn!" All of the bunnies' eyes widened with surprise and Blue was revving up his engine and getting ready to race out of the house. "Hold on buddy," Agent Rupert said. "Let's take a moment and figure out how we are going to approach this as a team, but we must do so quickly, because we likely don't have much time before the thief figures out something has gone wrong."

Cashew suddenly bolted out of the room and was gone for about a minute and then came running back in, and before he could say anything Blue yelled out, "Look! It's Secret Macadamia!" Secret Macadamia stopped in delight and smiled widely at Blue, happy to be recognized even if he was the Master of Disguises. "I've devised a plan," he said proudly. "We obviously must sneak up on the barn to catch the Carrot Thief, so we must be well-disguised when we do so." The collective excitement in the room turned up a notch at the mention of disguises, although Blue, after their last attempt, was a little nervous about trying it again. "We must disguise ourselves as… (again there was a dramatic pause)…CARROTS!" The silence in the room was deafening as the bunnies tried to understand how they could possibly disguise themselves as carrots when they were actually bunnies. Dino, still excited by the idea of catching her first thief, was the first to come up with an idea. "Agent Rupert. This might not be the best idea, but did I happen to notice some orange carpeting in your hoomins' litter box room (this is how bunnies referred to bathrooms)." Smurfy spoke up quickly! "Oh! Yes! I'm an expert at carpet removal according to my hoomins, so I could chew up separate pieces that we could roll ourselves in so we look like carrots." All the rest of the bunnies quickly volunteered to assist with the carpet chewing because, as we have previously learned, there is nothing like a bit of good bunstruction to make a bunny happy. With that, the bunnies all got to work.

CHAPTER EIGHT

It didn't take long before the bunnies had each chewed up enough pieces of orange carpet to wrap around themselves for the mission (bunstruction can happen very quickly when you are a focused bunny). They turned to Secret Macadamia for the next set of instructions but it turned out, besides wrapping themselves in orange carpet, he hadn't thought much about next steps. After all, he was simply the Master of Disguises and not plans. Thankfully, Dino had thought about it and she laid out a plan where the bunnies would all start at the top of the hill, wrap themselves in the orange carpet, and roll down the hill where they would all eventually bump into the barn at the bottom. "Once the Carrot Thief hears the bumping, he will think his carrots have arrived, come out of the barn, and we will take off our disguises and apprehend him!" she finished excitedly. There was much thumping and binkying as the bunnies celebrated what they thought was a most excellent plan. Agent Rupert packed his handcuffs just to be on the safe side.

The bunnies grabbed their pieces of carpet and silently headed to the hill above the barn. They could see a light burning through one of the windows on the side and could see a shadow passing in front of it, so it seemed the Carrot Thief was there and likely agitated that his carrots hadn't arrived. Blue, not wanting to seem afraid, was the first bunny to wrap himself up. He grabbed the corner of the carpet, gave a half turn and flopped down onto the ground, rolling himself up like a bunny burrito. "Are you ok in there Blue?" Smurfy asked. "Yes. I'm just fine and ready to roll!" came the muffled reply and the others giggled, because they actually were going to roll down the hill. The other bunnies quickly began wrapping and rolling in their carpet except for Agent Rupert. The group had agreed that he would hide behind the corner of the barn and come out with the handcuffs when the bunnies unrolled themselves in front of the unsuspecting Carrot Thief. At the last minute, Dino reached out and grabbed a tree branch with some leaves and stuck it into the top of her carpet carrot. After doing so she heard, "It is I, Secret Macadamia, and I wholeheartedly approve of the addition to your disguise. Now you really look like a carrot with a top!" With that, he quickly distributed branches to the other bunnies who lay still waiting for the word to roll.

At the bottom of the hill, Agent Rupert flashed his cell phone flashlight three times, indicating that it was time to roll, and Cashew (they didn't know where Secret Macadamia had gotten off to) gently pushed the bunnies down the hill. "Good luck, Blue," Cashew whispered, to which he heard a quiet "Thank you, friend." The bunnies rolled slowly at first and suddenly the hill got a little steeper and they started rolling faster and faster. Agent Rupert worried that they were going to crash through the barn, but they slowed down and one after another they thumped into the barn wall. Thump. Thump. Thump. And then they waited. Before long, the barn door slowly began to open and a small orange lion hopped out. "Wait a minute," Agent Rupert thought to himself, "lions don't hop." He waited, more curious than alarmed at this point, as the small orange lion got closer to the carpet carrots and paused.

Before Agent Rupert could even step into the light, Dino quickly unfurled herself and hopped up, saying, "Ah-ha! We have captured you Carrot Thief!" Dino truly was very excited to capture the thief. The Carrot Thief let out a scream as Smurfy rolled out of his carpeting and they all looked toward Blue but didn't see any activity. As it turns out, Blue was sort of stuck in his carpet carrot, but they all gave a little scream of surprise when they heard "It is I, Secret Macadamia, Master of Disguises, and I have come with the Super Bunny Club to apprehend you using some really fantastic disguises!" While

this announcement was being made, Blue finally got himself going and accidentally unrolled himself right into the small orange lion, who gave a shriek, a thump, and a poop and turned to run, right into Agent Rupert.

"Stop right there, small orange lion!" he said firmly and shone his flashlight on the thief while getting his handcuffs ready. As the light shone upon the small orange form Dino let out a horrified yelp. "Dodo? Is that you?" she said in shock. The small orange lion lifted his head and they all realized that this was no lion but rather a lion-head rabbit. This is a breed of bunny with a simply stunning mane of hair that reminds hoomins of lions, hence the name. Dodo still tried to run and Dino quickly hopped in front of him, and in a typical big sister voice said, "Make one more move Dodo and I am SO telling mommy and daddy that you are out after curfew!" It all made for a pretty awkward situation for the other bunnies who didn't know exactly what they should do or where they should look as this family drama unfolded in front of them.

Secret Macadamia was the first one to come forward and asked, "Is this a lion disguised as a bunny or a bunny disguised as a lion? Either way it's simply a smashing disguise." The other bunnies couldn't help but agree but Dino shook her head angrily. "This is no lion. This is my little brother Dodo, who my parents adopted so I would have some company, but he is NOT supposed to be out and he is definitely NOT supposed to fly his drones without a hoomin present." Dodo tried to make himself look even smaller as he faced the anger of his sister. Agent Rupert, wanting to put a stop to things before they escalated, stepped in and said gently, "Dodo, can you tell us why you were stealing carrots?" Dodo looked around fearfully and said, so quietly that the other bunnies all had to put their ears forward to hear him, "I…I…I…wanted to show Dino that I could be a good spy bunny too." Blue, who very much knew how it felt to want to be a spy bunny, stepped forward and spoke up. "Dodo, what you did was not very nice and stealing is never right, but we appreciate you being honest with us." The other bunnies nodded in agreement, but the fact remained that there were still many stolen carrots in the barn and many angry bunnies across the land.

Smurfy, who had to admit to himself he was a little disappointed that it wasn't a more dramatic apprehension of a real thief, still wanted to come up with a solution and suggested that Dodo return the carrots. "Perhaps you could write an anonymous apology note, Dodo. I'm sure the bunnies won't care as long as their carrots are back." This was a very true statement as bunnies are primarily interested in their treats regardless of the circumstances under which they are given. Dodo looked quite concerned and his eyes filled with tears at this suggestion, as he was actually a pretty good thief and had stolen quite a few carrots so the task ahead of him was a long and large one. Dino, who had already softened towards her little brother's mistake, volunteered to teleport with him to return them and the rest of the Super Bunny Club also agreed to pitch in. "Can

I be a spy bunny now?" Dodo asked and Dino gave him an exasperated look that only a big sister could give.

Agent Rupert jumped in and said, "Well Dodo, stealing is never right even if you had the best intentions, but it seems like your punishment is a fair one. I am sure you learned a powerful lesson tonight about right versus wrong so I will let the other members of the Super Bunny Club vote on your membership." Blue hopped up next to Dodo and added, "Dodo, throughout my adventures as a spy bunny, I too have learned some valuable lessons and, in fact, have been turning them into rules for the Club (Blue was started to get pretty proud of the rules and all the good lessons he had been learning). I vote yes to you becoming a junior spy bunny, as we can definitely use your help with drones, but only if you can write the sixth rule for the Super Bunny Club."

Dodo only hesitated a second before loudly pronouncing, "I now give to you the **Sixth Rule of the Super Bunny Club: It is ok to make mistakes as long as you are honest and take responsibility for your actions!**" Dino beamed proudly at her little brother and raised her paw for her vote yes quickly followed by Smurfy, Agent Rupert and Secret…wait, where was Secret Macadamia? They would tell him later what had happened but either way, that was the night that the Super Bunny Club gained a small new orange junior spy bunny who still looked an awful lot like a lion.

CHAPTER NINE

By the time the Super Bunny Club had transported around to return all the carrots, it was once again starting to get light outside and it was time for them to head back to their own homes. No one to this day is still quite sure how it happened, but there was a bit of a mix up when the bunnies tried to teleport home. Thankfully Cashew/Secret Macadamia was able to make it back to his home and Dodo was already home because Dino sent him there as soon as his carrots were delivered. The rest of the Super Bunny Club, however, were not so lucky. There was the usual buzzing and **WHOOSH**, but when Blue opened his eyes, he was still sitting in Agent Rupert's cage although he was very much alone. At the same time, Dino was opening her eyes in Blue's cage and Smurfy had somehow ended up at Dino's house and Agent Rupert found himself outside in Smurfy's castle. It was, as the bunnies will forever refer to it, The Great Bunny Shakeup.

Blue was immediately in a panic. He thumped and knew there was no one there to hear him, but deep down he worried that he had messed up the teleporting. You see, just as he was starting to teleport, he saw a small piece of basil in Agent Rupert's bowl and thought it might be nice to have a snack during the trip. As he leaned forward to snatch the basil with his teeth, he thought he felt something give him a little push from behind (which may or may not have been Agent Rupert). This caused him to slip a little and he felt himself bump into Dino, who then bumped into Smurfy, who then bumped into Agent Rupert, thereby bumping them all out of their correct teleportation paths. Because the hoomins were starting to deliver breakfast, none of them had time to contact each other, so they were on their own for the moment.

As Blue's mommy entered the room, Dino flopped onto her side and raised her head sleepily, pretending that the door opening had awakened her. "Now that's interesting," Blue's mommy said. "You never sleep on the floor of your cage, Blue. You always sleep on your little ledge." With that Dino quickly hopped up onto the ledge and eyed the hoomin warily, but then a large leaf of lettuce was placed in front of her and a small sprinkling of pellets (bunnies love pellets but aren't allowed to have that many) and a little baby carrot.

Before she could help herself Dino bounced out of the cage and began binkying around them room (because bunnies often binky at breakfast time). Blue's mommy laughed and Dino, loving the attention, ran in circles around the mommy hoomin's feet until she was slightly dizzy. "Go ahead and start eating your breakfast, Blue before I leave for work." Blue's mommy said kindly. Dino, always the trickster, pretended she didn't know the breakfast was there and looked around with confusion. She suppressed a giggle as Blue's mommy looked down on her with concern. "What's the matter, Blue? Your breakfast is right there! Aren't you hungry?" Dino, happy that her trick was working, simply sat there ignoring the breakfast and hoping for a treat for being such an amusing bunny. "Hmmmm," Blue's mommy said with concern. "I hope you are not getting sick. You never ignore your breakfast. If you are not better later, I may have to take you to the vet." With that she gave the surprised Dino a little pet on the head and exited the room. "Oh no. Oh no. Oh no," worried Dino. "I was just trying to be funny. I play this game with my hoomins every morning and they just laugh. I can't go to the vet. They will figure out I'm a girl and not Blue and then the hoomin is going to get upset." She kept worrying to herself but while eating breakfast because, after all, every bunny enjoys a nice breakfast.

Things weren't going much better for Smurfy but at least he had Dodo to help keep him company. Smurfy could hear the hoomins moving around in the other room and asked Dodo how his sister acts in the morning. Dodo laughed and said, "She usually pretends to ignore her food, because it makes the hoomins laugh and then they pick her up and cuddle us and give us kisses goodbye before they leave for work." Smurfy stared with horror. Before he could tell Dodo that he didn't like to be picked up (some bunnies are four-paws-on-the-ground-at-all-times kind of bunnies), the door opened and the mommy came in with breakfast. Dodo stood up hungrily and his mommy combed his hair with her fingers thinking he had some crazy bed head but really, Dodo just hadn't groomed himself after his big adventure. Meanwhile, Smurfy immediately ran over to the food, picked up a piece of parsley and ran around the room with it at top speed. Dino's mommy just stopped and stared because Dino always pretended to ignore her breakfast making her mommy laugh. Smurfy, on the other hand, loved to take his food and run (Smurfy pretty much never stopped moving) but he stopped quickly when he saw the concerned look in the mommy's eyes. He ran back to the food bowl and began eating his parsley and the mommy leaned down and gave him a rub on the head, so he thought the worst was over.

Suddenly Dodo, who was eating next to him, got lifted up in the air and was being cuddled in his mommy's arms. As if that wasn't scary enough, he actually seemed to like it! Just as quickly she put him down and before Smurfy could run, he found himself being scooped up for his morning cuddle as well. That's when things got a little ugly. Smurfy immediately began to struggle and kick and claw at Dino's mommy and launched himself out of her arms and quickly ran behind a chair to hide. He could see the mommy looking at the scratches on her hands and overheard her saying to herself as she left, "That is not like you Dino. I hope you are ok, otherwise I will have to take you to the vet later." Smurfy's eyes widened in fear because no bunny liked the vet, but he ran back to finish his parsley because it seemed silly to let a good breakfast go to waste.

Meanwhile, back at Smurfy's castle, Agent Rupert wasn't terribly concerned about the switch in homes as he was obviously a more experienced spy bunny and was up for the challenge. In fact, he engineered the entire Shakeup as it was a good training opportunity and a lesson on hiding in plain sight. So, he stretched out in the sun and closed his eyes. When Smurfy's daddy appeared with breakfast, Agent Rupert opened his eyes, gave a big yawn, and hopped over to see what was being served. He gratefully accepted the fresh basil and mint leaves and let the hoomin pet him on the head. He kept happily munching away and enjoying the attention when he heard Smurfy's daddy talking to his mommy who had also come out into the yard. "I think there might be something wrong with Smurfy," he said with concern. Smurfy's mommy immediately picked up on the behavior change and said worriedly, "Why is he just sitting there eating breakfast and not running around? And did I see him actually letting you pet him this morning too?" Agent Rupert stopped in mid-chew. Apparently Smurfy was a bit more active in the morning so he quickly swallowed the mint leaf he was eating and began running in circles around the castle. "Why is he doing that?!" Smurfy's daddy exclaimed nervously. "He never runs around his castle. He always runs up and down his ramp and in and out of his castle. Do you suppose something is wrong?"

Agent Rupert came skidding to a halt and flew up the ramp and into the castle as quickly as he could. He was getting ready to come out when he heard the mommy remark that

Smurfy never left his breakfast unfinished before beginning his morning sprints so he quickly ran back out of the castle and back to the mint and basil. This was all getting a bit exhausting as even Agent Rupert hadn't realized how closely hoomins watched their bunnies. It seemed the danger had passed until he heard Smurfy's daddy mention that he might take him to the vet later if he was still acting strangely. Agent Rupert froze, as even the most experienced spy bunnies didn't like the vet, but he decided to finish his breakfast before considering the situation further.

Back at Agent Rupert's house, things were still pretty quiet and Blue sat very very still trying to figure out his plan for how to act when the hoomins came in. Eventually he heard them waking up and moving around and he tried to think like Agent Rupert. What would he do in the morning? Blue thought about it and suddenly had a brilliant idea. At his house, Blue had a leather chair and an ottoman that clearly must have been put there for him because it was his room. Blue had immediately claimed the chair as his own and always sat regally upon it thinking "This is MY chair. This is MY ottoman."

There are actually a lot of things that bunnies think they own. They think of things as MY. MY room, MY chair, MY carpet, MY blanket, MY queen-sized bed. The concept of MY is something that hoomins don't seem to understand and that always confuses bunnies as they feel they make their ownership claims pretty clear. The bunnies suspect that part of the problem is that hoomins don't understand the concept of chinning. You see, bunnies have scent glands under their chin, so when they rub their chin on something, they considered it chinned and now owned by them. Most bunnies have pretty much chinned everything in their homes so it is very confusing to them when they are told "No, don't bite or chew on that!" They wonder why they can't do so, as clearly the item is theirs to do with as they please.

So, in the spirit of MY and chinning, Blue scampered out of Agent Rupert's cage and soared into the air making a perfect landing on the chair across the room. He sat up proudly and fearlessly (at least he pretended to be fearless) but tensed up when he heard the footsteps getting closer. The door slowly opened and Agent Rupert's daddy stuck his head around it and quickly and sternly said "Hey! You know the rules buddy. No sitting on that chair. That's MY chair and I can't have you getting hair on it or scratching it with your claws. Down please."

Blue sat in stunned silence. He had clearly claimed the chair as his, as he assumed Agent Rupert must have done, and couldn't believe what he was hearing. Besides, Agent Rupert was an experienced spy bunny, so Blue expected his hoomins to treat him with a little more respect. With that, Blue felt he needed to stand up for his friend's rights and hugged his body closer to the chair. "Down Rupie. Down," the daddy demanded and snapped his fingers. Blue's ears went back and he grew even flatter (while reminding himself to tease Agent Rupert later about his nickname Rupie). The daddy seemed to sense there was a challenge on as it was clear Blue was not going to back down or get down. If there was one thing he felt strongly about, it was ownership of a chair. "Agent Rupert. You come down off the chair right now," the daddy said more sternly. Blue gave a little growl (yes, bunnies can growl) and lunged forward a little. "Someone is cranky today!" the daddy said with surprise. "But I know how to solve this problem. Maybe your favorite treat will help convince you to get down."

The daddy left and Blue felt sort of bad for acting a little aggressively, but it was ownership of a chair we were talking about. As quickly as he had left the daddy returned holding something behind his back. Blue felt a little proud at that moment to see his confidence being rewarded with a treat so he stuck his nose out tentatively. That is when things got a little crazy. The daddy slowly took out the treat and held it in front of Blue and it was a BUHNAHNUH! Blue gave a little scream (as we all know buhnahnuhs are sceery to Blue) and he took off running. In fact, he ran faster than he had ever run before and flew out the back door, down the steps and into the shed in the garden. Sadly, that hiding place didn't quite work out as he had hoped as there was a giant spider in the shed (bunnies are similar to us in some ways when it comes to spiders), so Blue gave another little shriek and ran out of the shed and right into the arms of Agent Rupert's daddy who declared right then and there that he was taking him to the vet. What Blue did not yet know, was that all of the Super Bunny Club members had found themselves under increased scrutiny and threatened with the same trip.

CHAPTER TEN

Veterinarians are very wise when it comes to taking care of animals of all types and sizes, but most bunnies do not enjoy their trips to the vet. In fact, bunnies refer to vets and any medical professionals as "White Coats," although Cashew/Secret Macadamia referred to them as "Proddy Hoomins," because they always seemed to poke and prod bunnies during their visits. Needless to say, Blue was not happy when he was put into a carrier and shuttled off to the nearest White Coat because of his seemingly uncharacteristic behavior.

While in the carrier, Blue anxiously checked his PictoBun account to see if any of the other spy bunnies had reached out with suggestions on how they were handling the Great Bunny Shakeup. There were no posts from anyone, so Blue didn't know if that was a good thing or a bad thing. He did know he was still on his own for the moment. Once at the vet's office, the technician took him into the back so they could observe him for a while. Blue sat anxiously and very still in a little kennel fearing that any behavior would be the wrong behavior. It was while he was sitting quietly that he heard sniffling coming from the cage next to him. Soon it sounded like full on crying. "Hello?" Blue asked tentatively. "Are you ok over there?" There was only silence in response but soon enough the sniffling started again so Blue once again asked, "Hello? I can hear you crying so something must be wrong. Why are you so upset?" This time a small voice answered him saying, "I am not (hiccup!) ok at all (hiccup!)." It seemed Blue's neighbor had gotten the hiccups during his crying jag so Blue gently suggested he drink some water and then talk.

After his neighbor had finished drinking Blue politely resumed the conversation. "My name is Blue and I am a spy bunny and member of the Super Bunny Club (he still puffed up with pride at saying this), so perhaps I can be of some assistance?" Blue wasn't actually sure what he could do from a locked cage but he figured he should at least ask. His neighbor answered back, "My name is Nugget and I am a gray and white Angora rabbit and I am all alone!" With that the crying started but Blue was getting a better idea of what his neighbor looked like. He knew that Angora rabbits had very very long fur and were quite beautiful but also quite emotional it seemed. "Why are you here, Nugget? I know it can be sceery to go to the White Coats but why are you crying? Did they do something to make you cry?" Blue asked with some concern, some of which was for himself. "No. They have been very nice to me but I am crying because I am all alone. Someone found me in a park because my hoomins didn't realize how much work taking care of a bunny with hair like mine can be, so they abandoned me!" With that the crying started anew.

Blue realized that this was a serious situation indeed, as there were many bunnies out there in need of good homes but a bunny with Angora hair could be a problem if the right hoomin adopters couldn't be found. "Don't worry, Nugget," Blue said with more conviction than he actually felt. "The Super Bunny Club will rescue you and help to find a new and better hoomin to take care of you! I just have to figure out how to get out of here first." Blue then explained the teleporting shakeup and how Agent Rupert's daddy brought him here because he didn't do a very good job at impersonating Rupert. Blue was actually a little embarrassed about this, because he felt he should have done a better job fitting in but there was nothing he could do about that at the moment. He quickly decided that when the White Coats came in with Agent Rupert's daddy, he would just be extra docile and extra cute to make them think there was nothing wrong with him. Sure enough, the White Coat came in and declared Blue (er, Agent Rupert) to be a healthy bunny and before long, Blue was on his way with promises to the very fluffy Nugget that he and the team would be back that night.

CHAPTER ELEVEN

Once back at Agent Rupert's house, Blue was exhausted from his trip to the White Coats and from the evening's previous adventure so he got into Rupert's cage and fell fast asleep. The other members of the Super Bunny Club had also realized that sleep was the best protection and they too were napping. Finally, nighttime came again and they were all quick to teleport back to Agent Rupert's to compare stories. Dino reported that she had ignored breakfast in an attempt to be cute and that Blue's mommy had immediately thought something was wrong. Blue admitted that he normally just dove into breakfast, so he wasn't surprised at his mommy's confusion. Smurfy added that he had gotten picked up and cuddled and fought like an angry bull! Dino was sad that her mommy hoomin had gotten scratched but agreed that she loved her morning cuddles. Agent Rupert said that he had tried to just play it cool at Smurfy's house and hadn't realized that Smurfy was a very active bunny so he then overdid it with the running and confused the hoomins even more. The one thing they all agreed on was that hoomins were quite strange and honestly, a little annoying at times. They decided to make a list of things that irritated them about hoomins to make themselves feel better about the Great Bunny Shakeup. Smurfy took out a pencil and started writing:

Hoomins obviously do not understand that once a bunny comes into their lives, the bunny now owns everything the hoomin owned before, as clearly expressed with chinning and the claiming of objects such as MY chair.

Hoomins obviously do not understand that once a bunny comes into their lives they too now belong to the bunny and are expected to cater to the bunny's demands.

Hoomins obviously do not understand that breakfast and dinner are to be delivered at specific times and that weekends are no excuse for a late delivery of either meal.

Hoomins obviously do not understand that treats are to be given generously and not to be hidden in boxes or bags or puzzles as "enrichment" activities for the bunnies. Bunnies have very active social lives and do not need any "enrichment," thank you very much.

Hoomins obviously do not understand that petting only occurs on the bunny's terms and not when the hoomin decides they are interested. Not following this protocol can result in strong looks of disapproval, shunning, or even a warning nip.

Hoomins obviously do not understand Bunny Art and should be a little more respectful of walls that are chewed or property that is destroyed. Bunny Art should simply be appreciated and admired.

Hoomins obviously do not understand that how a bunny decorates his or her cage is completely up to the bunny and it is not appreciated at all when a hoomin comes in to clean. This creates much work for the bunny who must now spread hay all over again and put things back where they belong.

Hoomins obviously do not understand…

While Blue was enjoying the making the list, he finally couldn't hold in his story any longer. He felt that he had the most dramatic Shakeup experience because of the buhnahnuh, the spider, the White Coat visit, and, more importantly, he had also found a new mission for the Club. The bunnies finally stopped their list making and looked at Blue expectantly and he blurted out his story as fast as he could. "I got sceered by a buhnahnuh and then by a spider and then I confused Rupie's hoomins so much that I had to go to the White Coats!" The bunnies looked on with horror and sadness at their friend's unfortunate trip, but got a little less concerned and a little more interested as he continued. "At the White Coats I was extremely brave," Blue said proudly and perhaps a little exaggeratedly. "But more important than that, I have a new mission for us! At the White Coats' office I was next to a gray and white Angora bunny named Nugget who had been abandoned in a park because his coat was too much work for his hoomins. He was all alone and very sad so I told him the Super Bunny Club would come back to rescue him and find him a home." Blue looked excitedly at his fellow members thinking they would be happy to have another mission so quickly, but they all looked a little concerned.

"Blue," Agent Rupert began, "it's not easy to find homes for bunnies, especially ones with fancy hair like that. Plus we have never teleported to a White Coats' office before so I am not sure how we would get there and even if we did, how we would then find a home for Nugget." Blue immediately felt concerned that he had overpromised and also sad that they might not be able to find Nugget a forever home, but then Dino spoke up with a suggestion. "Well, I might be able to help with a home," she said. "There is a little girl who is a neighbor of ours and I heard her mommy tell my mommy that the little girl suffers from anxiety and that the doctor recommended an emotional support dog, but that they weren't allowed to have a dog. Maybe Nugget could live with her and when she brushes his hair it would help her to feel calm." The bunnies all thought this was an excellent idea and were anxious to rescue Nugget. Agent Rupert reminded them that they first needed to figure out how to teleport to the White Coats' office, which could be quite dangerous as there were hoomins in the office 24-hours a day. Although Blue was not completely confident in his offer, he promised his brothers and sister that he could get them there safely and the bunnies, who also were not completely confident in Blue's offer, agreed to try.

They gathered together in Agent Rupert's cage and Blue focused all his attention on safely getting them back to the vet's office and there came the familiar buzz and the **WHOOSH!** Before they knew it, they found themselves at the White Coats' office and IN A CAGE WITH A CAT! "Fighting positions everyone!" Agent Rupert shouted and the bunnies all growled, thumped, and prepared to lunge (bunnies can be quite fearsome when they need to be). They waited for the attack and the cat looked at them through half-opened eyes and yawned disinterestedly. "What on earth are the four of you doing?" he asked in a haughty and bored way that only a cat could pull off in a situation like this. "Be brave my friends," Agent Rupert said. "This very well could be a trick to lull us into complacency before he attacks. Hold your positions!" The cat replied sarcastically, "You know I can hear you right? I'm not going to attack, but I am a little curious about why four identical gray lop-eared bunnies are in my cage with me." Agent Rupert blushed sheepishly and explained to the cat that they were members of the Super Bunny Club and that they were there to save Nugget. The cat rolled his eyes (cats can be very rude) and flicked open the door of his cage, informing the bunnies that Nugget was on the bottom right, but that they should hurry because it was almost time for the nighttime check in, which meant that a White Coat could very well enter the room at any moment.

Agent Rupert thanked the cat and the bunnies ran off to fetch Nugget, who was peering curiously out of his cage. "Blue? Which one is you?" he asked. "Here I am, Nugget! These are my brothers Agent Rupert and Smurfy and my sister Dino and we are here to rescue you!" They could hear the cat laughing a few cages away but they proceeded to explain the plan to Nugget who would have agreed to anything at that point to get away from the White Coats (and the cat). After flipping open the cage latch, all four of the Super Bunny Club members squeezed into Nugget's cage and then buzz and **WHOOSH!** The bunnies all successfully landed back in Agent Rupert's cage. They quickly scampered into the garden where they proudly told Nugget the story of their last mission and the Great Carrot Heist while he enjoyed some fresh basil, mint, and a juicy carrot under the light of a summer moon.

CHAPTER TWELVE

Dino, always knowing when a fellow bun could use some kind words, snuggled up gently to Nugget and asked if he wanted to talk about what had happened to him at his last house. Nugget sighed deeply and his eyes welled up with tears, but he took another bite of carrot and explained. "Well, it all seemed like it started out positively. My hoomin loved my fuzzy ears and floofy bangs, but then my hair kept growing and growing and growing and she got tired of brushing me all the time. Then once my fur started to clump and knot, she finally gave up and left me in a park." At this point Nugget really started to cry and, to be honest, the rest of the bunnies' eyes got a little wet too, and they promised him they would help him to find a new home with loving hoomins. They also felt pretty guilty for complaining about their hoomins when they realized how lucky they were to have loving homes. Dino lightened the mood and explained their idea about the little girl down the street from her.

"Well Nugget, we hopefully have a solution for you," Dino said. "I have a neighbor who is a little girl who loves bunnies, but she suffers from anxiety. We were wondering if you would be interested in being a service bunny?" Nugget perked up but asked, "What is a service bunny?" Smurfy jumped in to explain. "Have you ever seen seeing eye dogs who help blind people get around? A service bunny is sort of the same, but all you really have to do is just be your best calming bunny self so she can pet and brush you when she feels anxious." Nugget agreed that this sounded like it might be the perfect solution but the spy bunnies now had to figure out how to introduce Nugget to the family. Dino explained that the mommy hoomin often took the little girl to the park in the afternoon and suggested that maybe Nugget could just hop out onto the playground and look cute. The bunnies all agreed that looking cute was pretty much the best way to get a hoomin to do anything, but Agent Rupert raised an interesting question.

"What if the hoomins think that Nugget is simply lost and don't want to take him in because they are worried that they are taking a bunny away from his home?" The bunnies all sat and pondered this very real scenario when Blue offered up an idea. "Maybe we could put a sign around Nugget's neck that says 'Free' so the hoomins understand that he was just left there." Luckily, Agent Rupert's daddy was an artist so they hopped onto his computer and quickly printed a sign that said 'Free' but then realized they had another problem. Going out together in the day time was going to be an issue for a bunch of spy bunnies that primarily operated at night when their hoomins were asleep.

"I can just go to the park tonight and hop out tomorrow when they come to play," Nugget offered. "I lived in a park for a whole month by myself, so one more night isn't going to be the worst thing in the world, especially when the outcome might be so positive." The Super Bunny Club wasn't sure that this was the best idea but couldn't argue with Nugget's thought process. "Dino," Agent Rupert began, "maybe you and Dodo could hop up onto the windowsill and livestream everything with your phone so we can make sure everything is going smoothly?" Dino was getting ready to respond but was cut off by a loud, "It is I, Secret Macadamia, and I am here to help with your problems!" Nugget gave out a little scream and a thump and dashed behind the garden shed and when he had calmed down and came out, Agent Rupert introduced him to Cashew, their computer support bunny. "But, I thought he just said he was Secret…" Blue cut him off. "Just go with it Nugget. Trust me on this one." So Nugget listened carefully as Cashew laid out a better plan that involved setting up cameras in the trees to capture every moment as it happened so they could livestream it on PictoBun. "This way all bunnies will become educated about this clever adoption scheme which may help other homeless bunnies in the future!" Cashew announced proudly.

The bunnies binkied with joy at the way the plan turned out, but before they teleported home, Blue cleared his throat and they turned to look at him. "Friends, I believe I am not the only one who felt a little guilty tonight about how we made fun of our hoomins earlier. The truth is, we are all very lucky to have safe and caring homes, which we are confident you will have tomorrow Nugget. And so, I would like to propose the **Seventh Rule of the Super Bunny Club: Practice gratitude and be thankful for all the good things in your life, big and small.** With that, the bunnies danced and binkied with glee, with maybe a poop here or there. Nugget then headed out with Cashew to set up the cameras while the rest of the bunnies teleported home with a newfound appreciation for their warm rooms and breakfast delivery service.

None of the Super Bunny Club could really sleep the rest of that night or the next day and were glued to their phones as the morning dragged on. Finally, the mommy hoomin came out of the house with the cutest little girl clutching, of all things, a stuffed bunny! The Super Bunny Club watched with nervous anticipation and with some pride at the number of viewers who were also watching the event live. Suddenly, out of the corner of the screen they saw Nugget hop into the picture and sit, in a very cute way, next to the swings where the hoomins were headed. "BUNNNNYYYYYY!" the little girl screamed and ran over to Nugget at top speed. Nugget tried hard to suppress his instincts and not run in fear, trying to simply trust in the Super Bunny Club's plan. Thankfully the mommy scooped up the little girl before she could yank on Nugget's hair, causing the little girl to cry (quite dramatically the bunnies all noticed) and thrash in her mommy's arms. Nugget, correctly sensing that this was his opportunity, stood up on his hind legs and wiggled his nose in a most appealing way.

The little girl and mommy looked down and slowly knelt next to Nugget and noticed his sign that said 'Free.' The little girl plopped down and slowly began petting him, her tears forgotten. The mommy noticed how much calmer the little girl became with this very calm bunny and picked up her phone.

After a few more minutes and a phone conversation with the daddy hoomin, the mommy knelt down and gently picked up Nugget, took the little girl by the hand, and headed home. The bunnies binkied and cried happy tears as Nugget looked over the mommy's shoulder and gave a little wave. Their plan had worked and the "Likes" on PictoBun were the highest they had ever been.

The members of the Super Bunny Club were still rejoicing when they noticed that first one camera came down and then another and then another! They watched as the livestream appeared to show a wild run through the park with much bumping and dragging and chattering in the background. Suddenly the cameras all went black and just as suddenly a text message appeared on the Super Bunny Club's phones from Agent Rupert with one word: SQUIRRELS.

CHAPTER THIRTEEN

After Nugget's rescue and the disturbing disappearance of the cameras, the day seemed to drag on as the bunnies were all anxious to teleport back to Agent Rupert's. Rupert was solemn as the bunnies appeared one by one (even Blue, who was finally getting the hang of this teleporting thing) and didn't waste any time getting right to business. "My brothers and sister. First, I must congratulate all of you on a job incredibly well done. In just a short time, you have helped a confused bunny, captured a carrot thief, and found a home for our new friend Nugget. My hope is that these experiences have provided enough of a foundation for you, as our next mission may be one of the most challenging yet." At this, the three spy bunnies all thumped a little bit because whatever it was, Agent Rupert was very serious about it.

Agent Rupert resumed. "We have spoken of 'bad guys' and 'thieves' during our time together, but I have not yet shared our relationship with one of the most conniving and worrisome creatures of all." He paused for dramatic effect. "Squirrels." The three bunnies all looked at each other with some confusion, as all of them had certainly seen squirrels but never thought of them as potential enemies of the Super Bunny Club. Again, Rupert continued. "For some time now, I have noticed that some of our electronic equipment seemed to be misplaced but after yesterday's events, I am now confident that they are not misplaced but have indeed been stolen by the squirrels." Smurfy interrupted with a question. "Are they spy squirrels Agent Rupert? Why on earth would they want to steal our things?" Rupert explained that this was part of the conundrum. He himself could not figure out why the squirrels were taking electronics, but he couldn't imagine it was for anything good. Blue just hoped electronics didn't extend to his race car and reminded himself to run a diagnostic check later. "Our mission moving forward is to develop a plan to stop this thievery and figure out the squirrels' motives, so we can put a stop to it once and for all," Agent Rupert announced. The bunnies all nodded in agreement but also agreed that thinking would be easier if they were in the garden eating some veggies, so they all trooped outside.

As he was thinking, Blue wandered the garden rows contemplating a plan and considering what he wanted to eat. He noticed some fresh basil growing, but the first plant was small so he decided to let it grow and continued down the row. The second plant was better, but also still a little small so he skipped this one and again continued down the row where he found an older and bigger plant that seemed perfect for snacking. As he took his first big bite, the idea hit him like a lighting bolt and he dashed back, mouth still full of basil, to his friends. "Wecanluremwitnuts!" he exclaimed. The bunnies looked at each other and then at Blue. "What did you just say?" Dino asked? "Wecanluremwitnuts!" Blue repeated and then realized his mouth was full. He swallowed and said more clearly, "We can lure them with nuts!" Smurfy immediately was on board with the plan. "Yes! Yes! Just like the Carrot Thief who was hunting for carrots, squirrels would definitely follow a trail of nuts and that would lead them right to us!"

It didn't take long for Agent Rupert to find a bag of nuts in his hoomins' apartment and the bunnies began laying out a row of nuts in one of the garden rows that ended up with a small pile in the shed. Now they had to figure out what to do once they had them in the shed. They began to think when a small brown ball of fur flew into the shed and declared, "It is I, Secret Macadamia, and I have a solution to your problem!" "How does he always know when to show up?" Blue asked and looked at Dino, who just shrugged and looked back to Secret Macadamia. He continued, "As the master of disguises, I will dress up as a squirrel to distract them, and while they are distracted by my most excellent disguise, the four of you will quickly pull the shed door closed and then we will inter-rogate them!" The bunnies agreed that it was a very good idea indeed, but wondered how Cashew, erm…Secret Macadamia, was going to transform himself into a squirrel. Agent Rupert just hoped that it didn't involve chewing up the gray carpeting in the living room.

Secret Macadamia hopped out of the shed and back in very quickly with a mouthful of hair. "Ivillusethithfer!" he said. "Oh here we go again," thought Smurfy. "What did you just say?" they asked in unison as Macadamia tried to spit out the mouthful of fur and repeated, "Ivillusethithfer!" And the bunnies just shook their heads at him. Finally after much spitting and commotion, Secret Macadamia got all the fur out of his mouth and said more clearly, "I will use this fur!" It turns out that Nugget, who really did shed a lot, had deposited clumps of fur around the garden during his visit, so the bunnies quickly gathered it all up and turned to ask Secret Macadamia how exactly he was going to make this work.

It turns out, bunnies are two things. They are very social animals who like to be around one another, and they are also very clean animals who like to groom themselves and each other. Secret Macadamia suggested that if all the bunnies got together and groomed him long enough, his fur would become wet and he would be able to roll around in the gray and white fur until he looked like a squirrel. It actually seemed crazy enough to work and heck, they hadn't thought orange carpet would make them look like carrots. And so, the bunnies began to lick and groom Secret Macadamia and his fur got wetter and wetter. Finally he threw himself down into the pile of fur, rolled around and around, and ended in a perfect dead bunny flop (the dead bunny flop is how rabbits like to get into their sleeping positions, but they often look dead and it terrifies their hoomins, which bunnies think is most amusing). When he stood up, they had to admit he didn't look like a bunny but it also wasn't clear that he looked like a squirrel. They decided to use a rubber band to hold his ears back and declared it the perfect touch. When he stood up on his back legs and ground his teeth together to imitate a chattering squirrel, they felt pretty good about their efforts and then hid themselves around the shed to wait (and thankfully the spider was nowhere to be seen).

It wasn't long before they heard a skittering and chattering sound coming from the garden. They weren't really surprised, as they figured the squirrels were emboldened by their theft yesterday and would continue with their dark mission tonight. Dino, who was peeking out of a crack in the shed wall, gave a quiet one thump signal to let them know the squirrels were close. Secret Macadamia prepared to emerge from his hiding spot as one, two, three, four gray squirrels all snuck into the shed on their bellies.

Once all four were in the shed, Secret Macadamia popped out from the darkness and when Blue saw him, he let out a scream as there was a large black spider sitting on Secret Macadamia's head. "Ahhhhhh!" Blue screamed! "EEEEEEE!" screamed the squirrels, and they began running and jumping around the shed like wild balls of gray lightning. Smurfy, Agent Rupert, and Secret Macadamia were also screaming and running, as was the spider who shot out the door into the night,

as Dino calmly closed the door behind him. She waited patiently and eventually all of the small gray animals in the shed came to a stop and looked at one another silently in a mix of fear, shock, and nervousness (mostly because they didn't know where the spider was) until Agent Rupert finally said, "I believe you have some explaining to do."

CHAPTER FOURTEEN

The squirrels, being rather brazen and cocky little animals, puffed up their chests and one of them said, "We don't have any explaining to do to a bunch of dumb rabbits. We are simply out foraging for nuts for the winter, and you need to let us out and then get out of our way." Secret Macadamia stepped forward, now just slightly damp with random tufts of gray and white fur attached to his body, and the squirrels took a step back as he did look a little unhinged at the moment. "My name is Cashew," he said calmly, "and as the computer technician for the Super Bunny Club, I believe you have some of my electronic equipment that I would like returned." The squirrels snickered and rolled their eyes and one said, "The Suuuuuper Bunny Club. The Super Dumb Bunny Club is what I would call you if you think we are giving anything back to you all." Smurfy and Blue bristled with anger and put their ears back and with a low growl, lunged forward, nipping at the squirrels' tails who elegantly dodged out of the way, sending Smurfy and

Blue tumbling into a rake. "Yah, look at you dumb bunnies. You don't even know how to attack someone. Come on boys, we're getting out of here." Stuffing their cheeks full of nuts, the squirrels prepared to leave but were met by Dino at the closed shed door.

"Eugene? Is that you?" Dino asked hesitantly as she peered at one of the squirrels in the dim shed. The squirrel at the head of the pack looked away and said, "I don't know anyone named Eugene, sweetheart, so you best be moving out of our way." Dino stared more carefully, walked over to the squirrel who just spoken, and said, "Oh no, I know it's you, Eugene. You know why I know? Because I found THESE on the floor!" She held out a pair of glasses that could only be described as nerdy, even though they were actually quite trendy these days, and the squirrel looked down at his feet. "I thought you looked familiar but I haven't seen you in years and didn't recognize you without your glasses. You were always being bullied about these glasses when we were growing up, and now I see you have become a bully yourself. Shame on you! And don't think I don't recognize you, Hubert, Norbert, and Cuthbert." Now all the squirrels looked down nervously and one of them began to cry.

Blue, recognizing how painful moments like these can be, hopped forward followed by the rest of the Super Bunny Club and gently held out his paw and said, "Hi. I'm Blue. I am a spy bunny and a race car driver. It's nice to meet you." The other bunnies piped in with their own introductions and the squirrels mumbled and murmured some embarrassed responses.

They finally all turned to face Dino, who had taken control of the situation. "So Eugene, do you want to tell us what's been going on? And the truth please with no bluster." Eugene sighed deeply and proceeded to tell them how the four squirrels had banded together because they were all being bullied and the other squirrels made fun of them. They decided if they were a group there would be strength in numbers. Dino paused and then asked, "Ok, I suppose I can see why this has all happened, but why were you trying to act like a tough guy?" The squirrels looked guiltily all over the room and anywhere but at Dino, who sat patiently with the other bunnies waiting for an answer. "We…we…we…thought if we were tough then the other squirrels would respect us more and leave us alone." "And has that happened?" Agent Rupert asked.

By now, Blue was hopping and shifting back and forth while the others were talking and they finally looked over at him and he looked like he was going to burst with information. "Go ahead Blue. I think you might want to say something?" teased Agent Rupert. "IthinkIjustthoughtofanotherrule!" he blurted out in one rushed sentence. "Ah, another Super Bunny Club Rule. That sounds like it might be appropriate. What is it?" Agent Rupert inquired. Blue paused for dramatic effect (it turns out bunnies are rather attached to these dramatic pauses) and then said, "The **Eighth Rule of the Super Bunny Club is: Treat others like you would like to be treated!**"

The bunnies clapped and binkied while the squirrels just looked more embarrassed until they too finally started laughing and doing some kind of strange spastic shuffle that the bunnies guessed was the equivalent of a binky. Dino followed up with the four squirrels saying, "You see boys, if you had just come to us to ask for help we gladly would have assisted. There are always going to be bullies in the world but that doesn't mean you should become bullies yourself. We all should remember the Eighth Rule moving forward, ok?" The squirrels nodded happily, but it was Cashew who finally added a little seriousness to the conversation by asking impatiently, "Ok this is all nice and fine, but can someone please explain to me why my electronic equipment was being stolen?" That's when the conversation got a little awkward.

CHAPTER FIFTEEN

At Cashew's question of the missing electronics, the squirrels first tried to pretend they didn't know what he was referring to but it was pretty obvious to everyone that this was not the case. Finally, Eugene admitted that they were pilfering the equipment because they thought they could somehow use it for a problem they were having. "And what's the problem?" Cashew asked, his nose wiggling with annoyance. "You wouldn't understand," Eugene replied. "It's not anything you should worry about anyway." Clearly whatever the problem was, it hit close to home for the squirrels so Dino, who still seemed to be in control of the situation, reminded the squirrels of their recently agreed upon rule. "Boys, as we just discussed, you treat your friends the way you want to be treated. In this case, you would want to help your friends if they have a problem, and we want to help. After all, we are the Super Bunny Club, so solving tough issues is what we do."

The squirrels briefly discussed it amongst themselves and came forward. "Ok, we will tell you what the problem is," Eugene said reluctantly, "but you can't make fun of us. You have to promise." The Super Bunny Club promised they would treat them respectfully no matter what, ears crossed (ears crossed is sort of like a pinkie swear for bunnies). "Well," Eugene said, eyes downcast, "Our problem is that when we hide our nuts for the winter, we can't find them again. I mean, eventually we find them," he said a little defensively, "but it takes us a long time and the other squirrels make fun of us." Agent Rupert smiled kindly and Blue let out a little snort of laughter, but Dino nudged him backwards quickly and gave him a warning look over her shoulder. "We thought if we stole some of your electronic equipment, we may be able to come up with some way of tracking them to save ourselves the embarrassment and the work."

"Well, Cashew," Agent Rupert turned to his friend, "it is your equipment they were taking. What do you propose to do? They have been honest with us and have taken responsibility for their actions." "Which is the Sixth Rule of the Super Bunny Club!" Blue piped in. Now all four gray bunnies and all four gray squirrels looked at Cashew, who was absentmindedly scratching his ear with his hind leg. After that, he began to groom himself and Smurfy cleared his throat. Cashew stopped cleaning himself and looked at Smurfy. "I am aware you are all waiting for me Smurfy. Sometimes I think better when I am taking a bath." The squirrels shifted nervously on their feet and Blue started to wonder if it would be rude to run into the garden for a quick snack when Cashew finally looked up and spoke. "This is actually quite a simple fix, but you squirrels are going to have to return my equipment for me to help you with your problem," he said. The squirrels readily agreed and Cashew nodded in response. "Well then, with that being agreed upon, here's the solution. All we need to do is build an app to track your nuts so you will always be able to find them. I am surprised you didn't think of this yourself."

Blue, who was still new to some of this technology and things like teleporting and livestreaming, didn't hesitate to ask for more details. Cashew, whose hoomin mommy was an app developer, was keen to explain how all of this would work to his eight gray audience members. He explained that first they would need to build a little computer hub in a tree. Then, when they found a nut, they would simply attach a small tracking chip that had GPS capabilities and something called Zigbee capabilities. When they buried the nut, it would be able to "talk" to the hub and they would be able to use an app on their phone to track their nuts. "I'm going to call it Nut Tracker 2.0!" Cashew proclaimed proudly (knowing his mommy hoomin would be super proud of him for paying attention to her work).

Blue, who had been trying hard to keep up with what was being said, looked at Cashew with a little confusion and said, "What's a Zigbee, Cashew?" Cashew, who had only heard his mommy use the word, wasn't quite sure himself, but he didn't hesitate in answering. "Why, they are bees of course. The bees get the signal from the nut and report it back to the hub, which the squirrels then see on the app!" He looked at the bunnies and squirrels to see if they had bought his explanation. "Zigging Bees!" Agent Rupert said with interest. "That is fascinating Cashew, and truly an excellent use of nature and our busy bee friends!" Cashew blushed with pleasure at the compliment while Blue called out that he wasn't going to have anything to do with bees. Two spider encounters in a 24-hour period had been enough for him, thank you very much. The bunnies and squirrels laughed with excitement and at Blue and at the most creative solution. In fact, there may have even been a poop or two on the shed floor after they all settled down, but no one would take responsibility for it.

The squirrels headed out to gather up the stolen electronic equipment and Cashew got his computer out and got right to work designing the app. Blue peered over his shoulder, as he felt a knowledge of computers probably would serve him well in the future. Dino and Smurfy started to clean up the things that had gotten knocked over during all the excitement about the spider and Agent Rupert headed off into the garden to read his text messages. He looked a little concerned, but when the others asked, he assured them everything was fine and encouraged them to keep working.

After the squirrels returned with the stolen equipment, Cashew yawned and closed his computer. "It's done!" he exclaimed with some excitement. "But it is getting light out and I need to do some beta testing, so I suggest that we all teleport home and meet here first thing tomorrow night." He continued, "Once the squirrels' phones are programmed, we can head to Dino's and set everything up. I will contact the bees first thing in the morning to make sure they are on board and ready to work tomorrow night." Everyone was tired but Blue couldn't help but ask, "Hey, how do you squirrels teleport anyway? It's not like you have cages." "That's for us to know and you to find out," they said with a little attitude and Blue shrugged. Even though they had come a long way in one night, they still were just squirrels.

CHAPTER

SIXTEEN

Once again, the daylight hours went by quickly as the bunnies were tired from another long night of activities. One by one, they all popped into Agent Rupert's and reported to the shed. The squirrels were waiting in the park by Dino's house already, so the Super Bunny Club just waited while Cashew did some final testing. "Maybe we should have a carrot tracker?" Blue tentatively offered, but when no one answered he realized that carrots basically stayed in one place but he still tried to think of other things to track. While Blue was thinking, Agent Rupert came into the shed once again looking carefully at his text messages and typing something in response. Smurfy looked over and asked, "Is everything ok Rupie? You haven't been able to keep your nose out of your phone, so I hope nothing is wrong." Agent Rupert, who had been distracted, looked up and quickly said, "No, no. Nothing is wrong, but I do need to talk to you this evening after we test Nut Tracker 2.0." The bunnies looked at each other nervously, but they trusted Agent Rupert implicitly and besides, it was time to head to Dino's.

The bunnies all got into Agent Rupert's cage, and then buzzing and **WHOOSH!** They plopped into Dino's and Dodo's cage in quick succession. Dodo was waiting for them impatiently, as he felt he should have been included in last evening's activities, but Dino reminded him that he was still a junior spy bunny in training. Dodo hid his eyes behind his long bangs but Dino licked him on the nose and told him he was obviously welcome to the park to test the app. With that, the bunnies, making sure the mommy and daddy hoomin were asleep, headed outside. Before anyone could head into the park, Blue took off running down the street at race car speed, and when they looked at where he had headed, they gave a little shout of joy when they saw Nugget peeking his head out of the door.

"Nugget! Nugget!" the bunnies exclaimed happily. "How are you? How is your new family and your job as a service bunny?" They noticed that Nugget now had a very short hair cut but long wispy ears and a small pink bow tied in one of them. He saw them looking at the bow and blushed, explaining that his little girl liked putting bows in his hair. "But I don't mind," he said proudly. "It is just part of my job as a service bunny." He told them that things were going very well and that his short hair cut made it easier for his hoomins to take care of him, but they left his ears long so he could keep his signature look.

"So is your little girl less anxious now?" Smurfy asked politely but curiously. "I think she is getting better with every day," replied Nugget. "It is going to be an adjustment for both of us, but it's worth the hard work because I now have a wonderful and safe home with lovely hoomins. I don't know what I would have done without you friends." His eyes teared up, which immediately made Blue's eyes tear up (he was a very sensitive bunny it turned out) and he looked at Agent Rupert.

"Agent Rupert," he asked. "May I announce another rule?" Rupert nodded in agreement and Blue stood up on his hind legs and proudly announced, "I now present to you the **Ninth Rule of the Super Bunny Club: Treasure your friendships because true friends are truly a treasure**." The bunnies all binkied with joy (and some tears) and Blue hugged each and every one of them, because in a short amount of time he had gone from being a sceered bunny in a new home to a race car driving spy bunny with the best friends in the world. The squirrels showed up and Eugene said rudely, "Wah. Wah. Wah. Look at all the dumb bunnies crying about their friendships." Dino thumped and flattened her ears and Eugene slowly backed away. "Suh-suh-suh-sorry Dino!" he immediately said with regret. "It's just that I have spent so long pretending to be a bully that I forget that I can just be myself with all of you now." The bunnies, understanding that Eugene was just a squirrel (the bunnies still had a bit of work to do on their own biases), quickly forgave him as Cashew motioned from the park for them to hurry over.

They all looked both ways but the street was very quiet at night and they hopped and skittered into the park. Cashew handed one of the squirrels a small white box and asked him to hide it up high in a hole in the tree. Norbert quickly scampered up the tree and stuck his head out after a few minutes and gave Cashew the thumbs up sign (which you might not think a squirrel can do, but they can in their own squirrel-like way). Cashew then handed the squirrels and the bunnies some nuts and small microchips to attach to the nuts, which they all

busily began applying, and then hid the marked nuts. While they were doing this, Cashew headed off into the bushes and was gone for quite some time. Dino was just about to get worried when she heard a noise from behind her and turned around with a little scream. "It is I, Secret Macadamia, Master of Disguises, and I am here to help solve your problems!" The squirrels, who had only experienced the disguises of Secret Macadamia once (and the squirrel disguise might not have been his best effort), also gave little squeals of terror and scampered up the tree. Standing before the bunnies and below the squirrels was a little brown bunny dressed up like a bee.

Agent Rupert was the first one to compose himself and said, "My goodness Secret Macadamia, that is quite the disguise you have put together. How ever did you come up with such a…uh…ummm…creative design?" Secret Macadamia blushed with happiness (bunnies do quite a bit of blushing as it turned out) and explained that he simply had chewed up a black plastic trash bag and put in holes for his head and paws. For the yellow stripes, he simply chewed off the yellow reflective tape on his daddy's bicycle safety vest and taped it to the bag. The bunnies murmured appreciatively at his creativity, while the squirrels warily climbed out of the trees and figured their best bet was to simply go along with the bunnies.

After receiving what he felt was an adequate amount of praise for his disguise, Secret Macadamia once again dashed off and then threw himself directly into and through a bush. The bunnies' mouths dropped open in shock but were even more surprised when he popped out on the other side of the bush with what appeared to be a very large swarm of bees chasing him. "Ahhh!" screamed Blue. "EEEEEE!" screamed the squirrels. Before anyone could turn and run though, Secret Macadamia was back in front of them with the now less angry looking swarm of bees hovering above him. "Friends, I would like you to meet Buzz and the rest of the gang. They are here to be our Zig Bees and will help to identify the location of the nuts." With that, the bees dispersed and honed right in on the hidden nuts and returned back to the tree with the white box inside. When that happened, the squirrels' phones pinged and their app gave them a small map to guide them. "Hooray! Yippee!" the squirrels shouted in delight, and the bunnies binkied with them to celebrate their success and the success of their friend Cashew.

"Hooray, Cashew, Hooray! Wait, Cashew?" The bunnies looked around and saw a small brown bunny dressed like a bee tearing at full speed toward a bush where he once again threw himself directly into it. This time, however, the bunny that popped out on the other side was not wearing a disguise and came running over and anxiously asked, "Did it work? Did the app work? Did the bees do their Zigging?" Eugene was just about to ask why on earth Cashew was asking that question when he had clearly been standing there dressed as a bee when Blue interrupted him. "Yes, Cashew, yes! The bees Zigged and the app pinged and the map popped up and the squirrels can now find their nuts! Secret Macadamia was here and did an excellent job bringing the bees over to assist. You should be very proud!" Cashew beamed with pride and happiness that everything had worked while the squirrels shook their heads. There were just some things, it seemed, that bunnies and squirrels were never going to understand about each other.

Lots of congratulations and well wishes were still being passed around when Agent Rupert's phone pinged rapidly with a series of text messages. The bunnies looked over at him and this time, instead of telling them everything was ok, he looked at them seriously and said, "Everyone. It is now my turn to congratulate all of you on a job well done. Cashew, you and Secret Macadamia did an amazing job creating Nut Tracker 2.0 and coordinating with the Zigging bees. And squirrels, I hope that you have all learned a few lessons and will learn how to treat others the way you would like to be treated from now on. I also hope you won't be stealing anything any time soon." The squirrels looked at each other awkwardly following the last sentence about stealing because they were squirrels after all, but nodded and assured Agent Rupert and the bunnies that they would do their best. "And now, Super Bunny Club members, we must be off. Nugget, we will hopefully see you soon friend. Congratulations on your new home and set of hoomins!" The bunnies hugged Nugget goodbye and headed back into Dino and Dodo's home for a very important meeting.

CHAPTER SEVENTEEN

Almost immediately, once the bunnies were back inside Dino and Dodo's house, Agent Rupert's phone began ringing and he quickly answered. They could only hear his side of the conversation, but he kept saying, "Yes, Sir. I understand, Sir. Of course, Sir. I couldn't agree more, Sir. Absolutely, Sir. Certainly nothing could be more important for our world today. Yes, Sir. We stand ready and willing to serve, Sir. I look forward to speaking with you soon with an update. Thank you Sir." He hung up and looked slowly up at the bunnies, who looked nervous, excited, sceered, and hungry all at once (it turns out bunnies are almost always a little hungry.) They settled down and grew silent as Agent Rupert began to speak.

"My dear Super Bunny Club members. I could not be more proud of the buns you have become. Not only have you professionally carried out numerous and varied important missions over a short amount of time, you have learned deep lessons about life and friendship. These lessons will act as a

103

powerful set of rules for us that will continue to enforce and strengthen both our missions and our values. Your work has not gone unnoticed." Blue looked over his shoulder to see who had noticed, but Agent Rupert cleared his throat and he quickly turned back around. "I have a most important and complex mission to present to you. I have been in nearly constant contact with our Presibun, George Washingbun, and he would like to temporarily detail us into his Secret Service for a mission so critical, it will shape and change the world as we know it." With that, Agent Rupert paused dramatically (bunnies really do love the dramatic pause), turned, and hopped into the other room.

The rest of the Super Bunny Club members were right behind him, and in the living room they found a large map of the world on the table in front of them. They stood up on their hind legs and rested their paws on the edge of the table to get a better look. Some of the areas of the map were blocked out in different colors. Some places were blue where hurricanes had recently struck, leaving many hoomins and their pets homeless. Other areas were colored orange, indicating locations where wildfires had been burning and destroying homes and taking lives, both hoomin and furry. Some spots on the map were brown where it had not rained in a long time, leaving the land dry and making it hard for both hoomins and animals to live well. Other parts of the world showed similar areas of natural disasters, but then there were other areas colored a deep dark red where wars were waged and hoomins and animals lived with fear and uncertainty.

The bunnies sighed with sadness to see such tragedies laid out before them on a single map. They simultaneously felt both grateful for the safe and comfortable lives they lived, but also deeply concerned and a little hopeless at the scope of the problems before them. "Um, why are you showing us this?" Blue asked timidly. Agent Rupert sighed deeply. "This map, where many buns live, clearly shows us the many tragedies that are happening across the planet. While we are only bunnies and cannot control nature or hoomin politics, we can create strength and hope within our fellow buns. That then is our challenge Secret Bunny Club. The Presibun would like us to unite all buns in love and create...The Bunited States." With that, Smurfy went right into a dead bunny flop, too overwhelmed to even process the news standing up.

Dino, who was always a little more calm and thoughtful, was the first to speak. "Agent Rupert, it is obviously an incredible honor to be tasked with such an important mission, but we are only four little gray lop-eared spy bunnies, and new spy bunnies at that. How could we possibly provide hope to bunnies all over the world and unite them into one Bunited States?" The bunnies were all quiet, including Secret Macadamia, who didn't even have a good disguise option for a task so large and important. Blue was the first to timidly offer a suggestion. "Agent Rupert, as you may remember, I initially had a very small problem teleporting to you successfully for our first meeting. While this was frustrating for me at the time, it did ultimately lead to the creation of the Second Rule of the Super

Bunny Club, which is that even if we look different, we are all the same inside so we need to treat each other with love and respect." Blue paused, waiting for some acknowledgment and congratulations at creating such a powerful and lovely rule, but when the bunnies just blinked at him, he quickly continued. "I guess what my journey is reminding me of is the great diversity of bunnies all across the world and our love for one another. Perhaps we could elect some bunny representatives from all of these places who could work together to find solutions to the world's problems."

Dino looked up from the map and said, "That's a bunderful idea Blue! Not even George Washingbun can do all of this on his own, but if we put all of our good ideas together using a diversity of opinions, that would be a powerful way to make progress. We could call it the Bunited Nations!" Agent Rupert smiled at his wise spy bunnies. Smurfy, who had risen back up to sitting, piped in. "We should have elections! This way all the buns can choose the bun they feel would best represent their opinions and every few years they could have elections again to mix things up a bit." The bunnies were now all getting excited at how their ideas were coming together. They turned to Cashew. "Cashew, do you think you could create an online voting system by location and then livestream the voting results so all bunnies can stay informed and knowledgeable about the process?" Agent Rupert asked. This was a huge undertaking for a small brown bunny, but Cashew, still feeling pretty good about himself following the launch of Nut Tracker 2.0, agreed to do his very best, which is all you can ever really agree to do.

With the basic framework of a plan in place, Agent Rupert placed a call to George Washingbun who agreed with the approach. He also asked the Super Bunny Club to think of a motto for the Bunited States and invited them to come to The Bun House in Canada (which is where the Presibun lives) in two weeks for a kickoff ceremony. Two weeks might not seem like a long time to set up a worldwide bunny government, but it turns out that bunnies are pretty good at keeping things simple and focusing at the task at hand (unlike hoomins, who bunnies felt complicated things more than was necessary). The bunnies were all pretty mentally and physically exhausted at this point, so they agreed to think on their own about a motto and got into Dino and Dodo's cage to teleport home.

🐰 CHAPTER EIGHTEEN

The next few days passed quickly for the bunnies. They were busy drafting framework documents for the Bunited States, setting up security details for the kickoff ceremony, monitoring the online campaigning, and preparing for the great election. Cashew had even enlisted the help of the squirrels for some of the computer work as they weren't spending as much time worrying about the location of their nuts and were quickly becoming proficient in computer programming. In fact, they had some ideas for Nut Tracker 3.0 that Cashew was excited to work on, but only after the elections had concluded. Before they knew it, the Great Bun Election Day had arrived and Agent Rupert gathered them together in his garden for an announcement.

The Super Bunny Club had never looked finer. Their coats were gleaming, their nails were trimmed (which was not an experience they enjoyed very much but tolerated for the special occasion), and their eyes sparkled with excitement.

They lined up as Agent Rupert did a final inspection and they watched him carefully as he gathered up small boxes with their names on them. The bunnies could barely contain their excitement (for if there was one thing a bunny loved, in addition to disguises, treats, and dramatic pauses, it was presents). They looked at Agent Rupert expectantly as he began to speak. "I will keep this short and sweet, as today is a most important day and there is still much work to be done. While your efforts as spy bunnies have been remarkable, what is truly outstanding are the efforts you have put in to create and serve the new Bunited States and all our fellow buns around the world. I have a gift for you today that, for me, symbolizes your full transition into the roles of Senior Spy Bunnies." At this, Dodo looked up expectantly and Agent Rupert winked at him to let him know he would no longer be considered a junior spy bunny.

He placed the presents in front of the bunnies who gleefully ripped at the paper with their teeth and then all paused to make sure they were opening their boxes at the same time. On the count of three the bunnies removed the lids, and embedded in dried carrot shavings (bunnies are very responsible when it comes to using sustainable packaging materials) were the perfect pair of sleek black sunglasses. They squealed with excitement, popped on their glasses, and binkied with much joy through the garden. Now they truly looked like experienced spy bunnies, although Blue was also secretly hoping that a race car upgrade might also be in his future if he worked hard enough. Agent Rupert thumped for their attention as they scurried back into line.

"I have one more surprise for you," he said with a serious face which quickly turned into a big grin. "We have some special transportation to go to the Bunited States kickoff event today. Mr. Presibun has sent Air Force Bun to fly us there in style!" The bunnies whooped and binkied and hurried out of the garden and down to the empty field where Air Force Bun was waiting for their arrival. They ran up the stairs, ooohing and ahhhing at the very large plane and quickly took their seats and fastened their seat belts. After the safety briefing had concluded, they took out their phones to check in on the status of the election results but all let out a simultaneous scream of surprise when a small brown form whirled into the cabin wearing a pilot's outfit announcing, "Surprise! It is I Secret Macadamia, Master of Disguises, and I am here to fly you to the event!"

"Oh no. No. No. No. NO," Blue said forcefully. "That is truly a masterful disguise Secret Macadamia but we need a real pilot to fly Air Force Bun." Agent Rupert giggled as Secret Macadamia looked smugly at Blue. "Perhaps this will make you feel better, young Blue," he said, and pulled out his professional pilot's license. "You didn't think I was just the Master of Disguises did you? A bun has to earn a living too you know." With that he sauntered off to the cockpit where he and his co-pilot (a bunny appropriately named Cessna), got the engines started and soon the Super Bunny Club, with sunglasses and all, were wheels up and on their way to the kickoff event.

CHAPTER NINETEEN

A few hours later, the Super Bunny Club was landing on the runway in Canada and Cashew reported that the elections had concluded and all over the world there were now bun representatives to serve in the Bunited Nations. While Cashew was making his announcement, Blue leaned over and whispered to Smurfy, "Um, who exactly is flying the plane if Cashew is standing back here?" Smurfy looked at him with confusion. "Who do you think? Secret Macadamia obviously." Blue's eyes widened, but before he could question this more the plane taxied to a stop and the bunnies gathered up their gear and deplaned. At the bottom of the stairs, they were met by the Press Secretary to George Washingbun, who brought them up to speed on the day's events. The bunnies all tried to play it cool as they were escorted to a stretch limousine bearing the license plates "PrezEBun" that would take them to The Bun House. "Where is Secret Macadamia now?" Blue whispered to Smurfy and Smurfy simply pointed to the driver who was wearing a jaunty driving hat, dark sunglasses, and an expensive looking black suit. Now it was Blue who giggled as they were whisked away.

The streets were lined with buns of all ages, sizes, and colors as they approached The Bun House, gleaming in white at the end of the road. There, on the front lawn, was a large stage and podium and off to the side, a large gray bunny sat with one ear up and one ear down, the trademark look of their very own Presibun, George Washingbun. As the Secret Bunny Club got out of the car, feeling rather cool in their sunglasses, they were all a little confused, Agent Rupert included, when they were led onto the stage by George Washingbun. The bunnies lining the streets had all now congregated on the lawn and large screens showed the livestream of the event being watched proudly by buns all over the world.

The Press Secretary stopped Blue, who was last in line, before he ascended onto the stage. "Blue, you have the new motto for the Bunited States written down, right?" Blue nodded that he did. "Excellent," she said smartly, "Buns around the world will look forward to hearing from you right after the Presibun says a few words." With that Blue's eyes widened, and before he could stop himself, a small poop popped out and rolled down the stairs. He looked around nervously to make sure no one had seen it. After all this event was live all over the world, but thankfully a commercial for a new brand of probiotic carrot juice was now playing on the screen (yes, even bunnies are forced to sit through commercials).

Agent Rupert, sensing Blue's nervous energy, turned around and said, "You can do this Blue. You have been the creative force behind all of our rules and were the inspiration for the new motto. Just speak from the heart." Blue gulped and nodded nervously and took his place on the stage as George Washingbun approached the podium. The crowd went wild with binkying and thumping (and a bit of pooping here and there, truth be told) as the Presibun raised his paws and asked for their attention. Thankfully, bunnies were very good at being silent and soon the only thing you could hear was the crackle of the microphone and Blue's tummy rumbling (but thankfully only the Super Bunny Club could hear that).

"Buns of the Bunited States!"the Presibun started and again, the crowd went wild celebrating their unification and this momentous day! He raised his paws for silence again. "Buns of the Bunited States. Today I join you in celebrating the successful creation of our unified world where all buns can come together to work on our problems, resolve our differences and create a stronger and better world for bunnies and all creatures alike." With this the crowd went wild thumping and chattering and again he raised his paws. "We have much work to do ahead of us and many challenges to face together but today I want to honor a very special group of bunnies. They have not only worked hard to keep us safe, but have also recognized the importance of our unity and were critical in getting us to where are today. It is my honor to present to you the Super Bunny Club who today, by Presibuntial appointment,

I am re-naming the Secret Super Bunny Club, now officially in charge of the security and safety of the Bunited States!" The Super Bunny Club members looked at each other in shock and surprise as the Presibun handed them very official and important looking badges and letters decreeing their new positions. The crowd cheered and whooped, as did bunnies all over the world who looked on proudly at four identical gray lop-eared bunnies who had made their dreams come true.

The Presibun returned to the podium and Blue's paws started to shake, for he knew his moment to speak had arrived. He barely heard the words of introduction that the Presibun was reading as he looked behind him with love and appreciation down the line of bunnies looking back at him. He looked at Agent Rupert who welcomed him warmly into the spy bunny world and who patiently guided him along the way. His brother Smurfy, who always supported his ideas and made them better, and his sister Dino and her brother Dodo, who believed in him and supported him even when he made mistakes. And then there was Cashew, er Secret Macadamia, who winked at him and gave him a paws up as he headed to the podium. Blue still wasn't sure he would ever really understand that situation, but it didn't matter at that moment for the love that emanated from his brothers and sister gave him the confidence he needed as he hopped behind the podium.

He gave one last glance to Agent Rupert, who mouthed, "You got this!" and Blue began to speak. "HELLO FRIENDS AND MEMBERS OF THE BUNITED STATES." The microphone squealed as Blue was speaking a little too loudly and a little too closely to it, so he jumped back a bit as the bunnies tittered affectionately. "I didn't know that I was going to be asked to speak today so I will be brief. I started this journey as a lonely bunny who was simply anxious to find his place in the world and someone who would believe in my dreams of being a race car driver. Through the power of the internet and PictoBun, I not only developed the confidence to pursue my dreams, I have also met bunnies from all over the world and have learned some powerful lessons about myself and life. These lessons have become the operating rules of the Super Bunny Club and will now serve as the guiding principles of the Bunited States. They have been posted to the official website of the Bunited States and there you will see the last and final rule. Today I proudly present the **Tenth Rule of the Super Bunny Club: Life is all about love.** The bunnies in the crowd and bunnies all over the world stomped, thumped, cheered, celebrated, and hugged one another. They were so proud to live in and be a part of the Bunited States, where everyone was respected and would be treated with love and kindness.

Blue turned away from the podium to celebrate with his brothers and sister, but the Presibun called out to him. "Blue, the motto! You forgot to announce the motto of the Bunited States!" Blue blushed furiously and quickly hopped back to the podium. The crowd silenced as he looked out at them with tears in his eyes. "My friends, I now present to you the official motto of the Bunited States: 'With Peace, Love, and Equality for All!' The bunnies around him all began to chant. "Peace, Love, and Equality! Peace, Love, and Equality! Peace, Love, and Equality!"

As the chanting continued, the Super Bunny Club members rushed to hug and celebrate with Blue as the Presibun congratulated all of them again for their fine work. Today was truly a monumental day and one the bunnies hoped would serve as a model for hoomins everywhere. It was clear that the celebrations were going to go on long into the night. Fine crystal glasses of carrot juice were now being passed around as the Super Bunny Club put on their sunglasses and posed for a photo. But wait, where was Agent Rupert? The bunnies looked around and saw him standing on the edge of the stage reading a text message with a concerned look on his face. He looked up at them and put on his sunglasses. It was already time for the Secret Super Bunny Club to get back to work (but maybe after a glass of carrot juice and a quick treat or two).

THE END

BUNCTIONARY

(like a dictionary, but better because it is only bunny-related terms)

Air Force Bun: The official airplane for carrying the Presibun of the Bunited States.

Binky: Any combinations of flips, hops, jumps, twists, or spins bunnies do when they are overjoyed.

Buhnahnuh: How bunnies spell *banana*.

Bunderful: Something that is extremely good, excellent, or marvelous. Similar to the word "wonderful," but better because it's bunderful.

The Bun House: The official Canadian workplace and home of the Presibun of the Bunited States.

Bunited Nations: An intergovernmental organization designed to create and maintain international peace and order. Made up of bunny representatives from all over the world.

Bunited States: The collection of all the places bunnies live all over the world. Sort of like the United States, but better because it's all bunnies everywhere.

Castle: How bunnies refer to their homes and hideaways.

Chinning: When bunnies rub their chins on items to claim them as their property. Bunnies have scent glands under their chins, so when they rub their chins on something, it leaves a scent for other bunnies to smell. Unfortunately, hoomins cannot smell this, which could be why they are often so confused about bunny ownership. See the word *MY*.

Dead bunny flop: Refers to the rather dramatic way bunnies flop into their sleeping positions, which often makes them look dead and terrifies their hoomins (which bunnies find rather amusing).

Ears crossed: Similar to a "pinky swear." Indicates a promise from one bunny to another.

Hoomin(s): How bunnies spell the word *human(s)*.

Hoppy: The bunny word for "happy." For example: Hoppy Birthday, Hoppy Holidays.

Lop-eared: Refers to bunnies whose ears drop down by the sides of their heads instead of standing straight up.

MY: This is an essential word to bunnies, as it refers to things that belong to them. It is capitalized because bunnies feel quite strongly about what belongs to them (which is pretty much everything a hoomin thinks they own). For example, MY chair, MY room, MY bed.

Pellets: Dry bunny food. Bunnies aren't actually supposed to eat a lot of pellets because hay is better for them, but they love them as a special treat.

Presibun: The bunny word for President, but better because it's a bunny.

Sceery: How bunnies spell the word *scary*.

Thumping: What bunnies do with their hind feet to communicate to other bunnies, especially when there is danger involved or they are trying to get another bunny's attention.

White Coats: How bunnies refer to veterinarians or other specialists who take care of animals.

MEET THE REAL SUPER BUNNY CLUB BUNNIES AND THEIR FRIENDS:

The adventures of the Super Bunny Club and their friends don't end just because this book did — you can follow the real live bunnies on their Instagram accounts. You may read about some of their spy adventures, but mostly you will hear them wondering why hoomins are so strange, eating treats (or trying to get treats), sleeping in the dead bunny flop, planning parties, complaining about bunny ownership issues, and, if you're lucky, binkying with joy!

Blue (@abunnynamedblue)
Agent Rupert (@agentrupert)
Dino and Dodo Bunster (@dino.dodo.bunster)
Smurfy (@smurfy_one)
Cashew (@monpetitcashew)
George Washingbun (@georgewashingbun)
Lucas (@lucas_the_lop)
Mochi (@mochibunny143)
Mr. Bigglesworth (@loafy_mrbigglesworth)

THE TEN RULES OF SUPER BUNNY CLUB!

1. Never give up on your dreams.

2. Even if we look different, we're all the same inside so we need to treat each other with love and respect.

3. Always be ready to help others, even if you don't understand why they are upset.

4. Everything in moderation. There is a time for fun and a time for work, but they must be balanced for you to accomplish all your goals.

5. Never assume anything about anyone. Get to know them first.

6. It is ok to make mistakes as long as you are honest and take responsibility for your actions!

7. Practice gratitude and be thankful for all the good things in your life, big and small.

8. Treat others like you would like to be treated!

9. Treasure your friendships because true friends are truly a treasure.

10. Life is all about love.

Acknowledgments

Most acknowledgment sections start by thanking the people who supported the author throughout their often arduous writing adventure. This is no different in my case, although I have both hoomins *and* bunnies to thank. First and always first, my husband Michael has always been my number one believer and supporter, no matter how daunting my dreams may sometimes seem. He has also been the one to give me the proverbial kick in the pants when needed, and trust me, sometimes it was needed. Besides his support of my writing habit, his acceptance (re: tolerance) of my love for all things bunny is the real reason we welcomed Blue into our home and let him take over what was once my office. I know the many bunstruction events, small and large (including the ones I may never have shared), try his patience and push his limits, but they are a testament of his pure and total love for me. *Thank you* will never begin to express how much this means to me. Plus, I'm sure deep down, Blue really is sorry for chewing up the chair legs (even though this will never be evident and is probably a not-quite-true statement).

I'm also ever grateful for my sister Mary Jo's endless enthusiasm and support for me generally and the Super Bunny Club. I and the bunnies appreciate it (although, let's be honest, the bunnies really just expect it). Huge thanks to the hoomins of Cashew/Secret Macadamia, Lucas, George Washing-bun, Mochi, and Mr. Bigglesworth for allowing me to include their bunnies in the story. You were some of Blue's first friends, and your support and friendship mean so much to us. A special shout-out to Cashew's mommy for helping to design Nut Tracker 2.0 — the squirrels (and I) are ever grateful.

Last, but definitely and most certainly not least, none of this would have been possible without the real life members of the Super Bunny Club and their amazing and wonderful hoomins. Their creative input, enthusiasm, and unwavering belief have kept my heart light, inspired me, and made me laugh on a daily basis. They are truly the heart of this book and will forever have a special place in my heart (and Blue's too). Finally, I need to thank all the other hoomins (and bunnies) from the world of Instagram. You are the most kindhearted, funny, and supportive group of individuals and you have buoyed me through sad hoomin times with your outpourings of warmth and compassion. You give me hope for the world. Many nose bumps (and treats) to you and your buns.

Long live the Bunited States.